LaPorte County Public
LaPorte, Indiana

D0005916

PILGRIMS DON'T WEAR *pink*

BY STEPHANIE KATE STROHM

G RAPHIA

Houghton Mifflin Harcourt

Boston New York 2012

*For Mom and Dad, who took me
to every museum I wanted
to visit, and for Ali,
who endured
them all*

Copyright © 2012 by Stephanie Kate Strohm

Lyrics to "Proud Mary" copyright © 1963 by Jondora Music.
Reprinted by permission of Hal Leonard Corporation.

All rights reserved. Published in the United States by Graphia, an imprint of
Houghton Mifflin Harcourt Publishing Company.

For information about permission to reproduce selections from this book,
write to Permissions, Houghton Mifflin Harcourt Publishing Company,
215 Park Avenue South, New York, New York 10003.

Graphia and the Graphia logo are registered trademarks of
Houghton Mifflin Harcourt Publishing Company.

www.hmhbooks.com
The text of this book is set in Garamond.
Book design by Carol Chu

Library of Congress Cataloging-in-Publication Data
Strohm, Stephanie Kate.
Pilgrims don't wear pink / by Stephanie Kate Strohm.
p. cm.
Summary: During a summer internship at a living history museum in Maine,
fashion-conscious Libby runs afoul of her roommate, investigates a haunted ship,
and seeks a romantic hero like those in the historical novels she loves.
ISBN 978-0-547-56459-3
[1. Interpersonal relations—Fiction. 2. Historical museums—Fiction. 3. Internship
programs—Fiction. 4. Haunted places—Fiction. 5. Maine—Fiction.] I. Title.
PZ7.S9188Pil 2012
[Fic]—dc22   2010045549

Manufactured in the United States of America
DOC 10 9 8 7 6 5 4 3 2 1
4500348245

"Please remind me again *why* you're going to pilgrim camp."

"Okay, first, it's not camp. It's a living history museum studies internship." I nestled my cell phone between my ear and my shoulder, trying to zip my suitcase closed with one hand. Definitely not working. "And second, ugh," I grunted. That zipper was like beyond stuck. "Like I've said about a million times, I'm not a pilgrim." I sat on the suitcase and tried to zipper it between my legs. "I'm an eighteenth-century New England colonist on the coastline of the territory now known as the state of Maine. It's a totally different thing. It's like mistaking Pucci for Gucci."

"Ugggghhhhhhhhhhhhhhhhhhhhhhhhhhhhhhhh."

"That better have been static, Dev, and not a sigh of disgust," I warned.

"Sorry, Libs," he said, "but you know my brain shuts down when you go all History Channel on me."

"*Mmmrph.*" The zipper still wasn't going anywhere. Did this mean I had to take out a pair of shoes? I couldn't lose a pair of shoes! I'd already pared down my two shoe racks to like the bare minimum of shoes necessary for basic human survival. Literally, there was only one pair of heels in there. *One.*

"It doesn't even make any sense," Dev continued. "Living history? What is that? Isn't that an oxymoron? Isn't all history . . . dead? Because it's in the past?"

"Dev, how many times have I explained this?"

"I wasn't paying attention before."

I sighed with frustration. "A living history museum is like a recreation of a village from a different time period, with all the museum workers dressed in costumes and doing chores or crafts or trades or whatever . . . Haven't you heard of Plimoth Plantation? Old Sturbridge Village? Colonial Williamsburg?"

"So sort of like Toontown in Disneyland, but not fun?"

"Sort of . . . No, wait! It's really fun!"

"It sounds really boring. You just used the word *trades*."

"No, it's fun, I promise! I mean, honestly, it kind of *is* like Disneyland," I said, reconsidering. "It's not like I'll actually be *living* in the eighteenth century. I mean, there are flushing toilets and a gift shop. It just *looks* like the eighteenth century. A sanitized, tourist-friendly eighteenth century. I'll be like an eighteenth-century Disney princess! Colonial Cinderella!" Oh, I could see it now. I had the perfect shade of lip-gloss to pull off that all-natural no-makeup makeup look.

"Libby, Libby, Libbeeeeee, listen to meeee," he whined. "We could have had so much fun together this summer! Not educational Disneyland fun. Real fun. In New York. *New York.* Not in Clamhole Harbor."

"It's Camden Harbor."

"Whatever." I could almost hear him shrug through the phone.

"Camden Harbor is really nice! It's so cute — like the cutest part of Maine ever. They filmed *Carousel* there, you know."

"They filmed what?"

"*Carousel*? The epic love story about mill workers and carnival barkers in a newly industrialized 1870s New England fishing village?" There's nothing I like better than when romance meets history. Nothing. "The Rodgers and Hammerstein musical?"

"Libby, not all the gays have an encyclopedic knowledge of the American musical theater. It's not like they hand you a DVD box set of the Rodgers and Hammerstein Collection in a Liza Minnelli souvenir tote bag when you come out."

"Well, they should. I'd totally be gay for a Liza Minnelli tote bag."

"I still don't understand why you didn't apply for the *Teen Mode* teen internship with me!"

Here we went again. We'd had this argument about a million times. Dev had entered an essay contest at *Teen Mode* and won a summer internship for high school students with his searing fashion exposé, "St. Paul-y-ester: So Yesterday."

"Um, Dev, I saw *The Devil Wears Prada*. There's no way I'd voluntarily subject myself to that. I'm not insane. And there's no way I would have gotten it even if I did apply! Not all of us benefit from the holy grail of diversity known as being perhaps the only gay Indian high-schooler in like all of Minnesota. How many straight blond girls do you think applied for that internship?"

"Libby, *The Devil Wears Prada* is *not* a documentary. How many times do we have to go over this?"

I squawked in protest. He ignored it.

"And you totally could have gotten the internship. You are almost as stylish as me, and that is not something I say lightly."

It was, in fact, this sense of style that had brought us together. As Dev had said the day we'd met almost three years ago in freshman English at St. Paul Academy, we were "an island of pastel in a sea of gray." Apparently, neither of us had gotten the memo that every other student at SPA would be clad in a gray North Face fleece. Who knew that private schools were where fabulous went to die? *Gossip Girl* it was not.

"Plus," he added thoughtfully, "*Teen Mode* probably needs some non-size-zero diversity! You could be their token size six."

"Thanks, Dev. That's sweet."

"Imagine it, Libby," he whispered seductively. "Right now, we could be running around the big city in Lanvin loafers and Prada pumps!"

"That is tempting, Dev," I agreed, "but it's your dream, not mine. Think about it. What does anyone who loves history secretly want? A time machine. That's all I've ever wanted, really. And since that's not possible, this is as close as I'll get. A real living history museum. Yes, Prada is nice, but I'll be spending the summer in full period costume, churning butter in a corset."

Technically, the term *corset* was more commonplace in the nineteenth century, but being perfectly accurate and saying "stays" might send Dev into history overload.

"And this is appealing?" he asked skeptically.

"Yes, Dev." I sighed.

"God, you're such a big nerd, sometimes I forget why I'm friends with you."

"Because no one else loves you enough to bake you butterscotch blondies as a *Project Runway* marathon snack." I shifted the cell phone to my other shoulder.

"Seriously. Seriously?" Dev asked again. "You're turning down Hermès for hoop skirts?"

"Your knowledge of fashion history is truly appalling. The

first patented hoop skirt didn't show up in the United States until 1846."

"Somehow I have a feeling *Teen Mode* doesn't care if I don't know what a bum roll is."

"Probably right," I agreed. Even though he'd only proved my point further, because bum rolls had gone out of fashion with Queen Elizabeth. The first one.

"What if I need you?" he demanded. "Do I have to send a carrier pigeon?"

"No, of course not." I tutted. "It's not a forced labor camp. I'll have my cell phone the whole time. I promise. It's not like anyone actually *thinks* it's the eighteenth century. They're historians, not Amish."

"Please, Libby," he begged, "don't leave me! There's no way I can make it through the summer without you."

"Oh, please, Dev. You made it through the first thirteen years of your life without me before I switched from public school to SPA. I think you'll be fine for three months. And you'll be in New York! Not home in St. Paul, but in glamorous New York! You'll come back with all these great stories and amazing clothes, and be all set to have the fiercest senior year *ever*. There'll be so much fabulous, you won't know what to do with yourself. Come on, you're gonna replace me with Anne Hathaway in like five minutes."

"Again, Libby, *The Devil Wears Prada*—not a documentary. Anne Hathaway does not, in fact, work at *Mode*. Or *Teen Mode*, which is where I'll be."

"You know what I meant."

"And if I'm replacing you with anyone," he interrupted, "it's that Hottie McSexypants Gucci Pour Homme model."

"You have my total permission to do that. Urgh!" There! I'd finally gotten my suitcase closed.

"Um, what was that?" Dev asked nervously.

"What?"

"That weird grunting noise. What are you doing over there?"

"Oh, I was having some trouble zipping my suitcase, but I did it."

"Hmm, let me guess. Wardrobe not quite fitting into that charming pink luggage set?"

"Maybe," I admitted.

"See?" he crowed triumphantly. "There's no way you can do this, Libby! You just can't! Pilgrims don't wear pink!"

"I don't wear that much pink!" I yelled into the phone. "And I'm not a pilgrim!"

He'd already hung up.

chapter one

"This is my closet?"

"No, this is *our* closet. This is your closet half."

Whatever it was, it was tragic. Not-*my*-closet was a rickety IKEA construction that had been sloppily partitioned in half. The empty half was tiny, and the other equally tiny half held a pair of cargo shorts, two T-shirts, and a polo shirt, which I gathered belonged to the girl currently eyeing my pink luggage with an air of disdain.

"That's a big suitcase. What did you bring?" She folded her arms across her frolicking otter T-shirt.

"Um, clothes and shoes and . . . stuff," I finished lamely, unzipping my suitcase. It exploded, shooting three sundresses and a polka dot bikini across the room.

My new roomie—a skinny, sallow girl with ashy brown hair—snorted and rolled her eyes.

"I'm Libby," I introduced myself, retrieving the bikini from the pastel quilt it had landed on across the room. Somehow they had managed to fit three beds in this tiny room. And the "closet," of course.

"Ashling," she responded, still standing in the middle of the room, watching me unpack.

"What a pretty name," I said, trying to be friendly, although I privately thought it sounded like the name of a gremlin. She already hated me, and all I'd done was accidentally turn my suitcase into a bikini launcher. Ashling turned and silently sat on her olive green bedspread, watching. No, "watching" was too benign — this was a full-on malevolent glare. I kept unpacking, stuffing as many hangers as possible into my tiny sliver of closet. The whole thing was beyond awkward. It felt like some sort of weird performance art piece: *Girl Unpacking, Series One.* Or a psychological experiment: *The Effects of Observation on Process of Unpacking. Case Study: Female, Age 17.* But the watching eyes making me the most uncomfortable weren't, in fact, Ashling's.

"I, um, love your cat posters," I said, trying again. I didn't love them. They were beyond hideous. There were cats all over the walls in Ashling's third of the room. One read HANG IN THERE! and had a tiny white kitten clinging to a branch. The other said FRIENDS and showed two kittens sharing a milk shake. And then there was a series of big-eyed kittens in flower pots staring at me. Creepy.

"Thanks. I love cats." Victory! She spoke, and this time it was only moderately hostile. "Do you have a cat?"

"Well, no. But I do really love animals. At home, in Minnesota, we have two dogs. Beagles. They're really cute. They're like part of the family; my mom's totally nuts about them. She keeps trying to get my dad to help her shoot them for the Hound Holiday Fun Photo Contest and stuff, because she says she needs him to run the tungsten light, but he has this thing against putting animals in sweaters, so . . ."

I trailed off as I caught sight of Ashling. Clearly, I'd made a fatal error in choosing the opposite side in the eternal dog vs. cat debate. The stare I received was so cold, I could feel icicles forming on my ears. Ashling picked up a book, pulled out her bookmark that read, I kid you not, "Cats Are Little People in Furry Suits!," and started reading. The door to communication had been slammed shut. Fine. At least I had tried. I started building a shoe tower at the bottom of my closet.

"Why do you have so many shoes?" Ashling arched an eyebrow over the top of her book, which appeared to be a Sisters of the Quilt Amish romance. I imagined it probably involved a lot of repression and meaningful glances beneath bonnets. Ashling, however, had clearly not gone the Amish route and decided to shun me, as the silent treatment had been short-lived.

"Well, you need a pair of shoes to go with every outfit." I balanced a pair of gladiator-inspired gold sandals on top of some cream ballet flats.

"*I* have a pair of shoes to go with every outfit."

"You do?" The bottom of her closet looked pretty empty to me.

"I don't know what you need all those for. You only need two pairs. Tevas. Sneakers. They go with everything."

I couldn't formulate a response. She did not seriously just say "Tevas" to me. Ashling returned to reading. Maybe Dev was right. Maybe I couldn't do this. If everyone in Camden Harbor thought Tevas were all-occasion footwear, I'd have to steal a canoe and paddle to New York. I'd reach the Hudson eventually, right?

"Hi." Someone else entered the room. Our third roommate, I surmised. "I'm Suze." She pushed her glasses up on her nose and stuck out her hand. "The Research and Curatorial intern." She sort of looked like a librarian, but not in a bad way—in a cool, sort of Velma from *Scooby-Doo* in plastic-framed glasses way.

"I'm Libby." I took her hand and smiled. "The Education and Interpretation intern."

"*I'm* the *real* Interpretation intern," Ashling piped up. The cat bookmark was back in and the book was closed. "Education and Interpretation is basically just babysitting the camp kids. Not *real* Historical Interpretation, like me," she sniffed.

"Ummm . . . okay," I said.

"Let me show you." Ashling motioned me over. "Suze has already seen this, but I think *you* could really learn something."

Suze raised her eyebrows and nodded, like I had no idea what I was getting myself into. Which I didn't. Ashling pulled a giant book out from under her bed. She patted the space next to her and I sat down. The cover read "My Historical Interpretation Scrapbook" in puffy letters and featured a black-and-white photo of a frowning Ashling in eighteenth-century dress.

"I am Susannah Fennyweather, the daughter of a whaler, and an aspiring suffragette," she explained.

"Suffragette? Aren't you like a hundred and twenty years early for that?" I asked. The term *suffragette* hadn't been coined until like 1906.

"I am a woman ahead of my times." No kidding. She was so ahead of her times, she might as well have been a cyborg. She flipped a page. It was a seemingly endless series of Ashling dressed as Susannah Fennyweather: in a garden, under a tree, with a parasol, by the water, at a ball, in the snow, on horseback, drinking tea, opening presents, eating a biscuit . . .

"Have you seen the rest of the house?" Suze asked, stopping the parade of Susannah Fennyweathers. Thank God.

"Just this little room." Just this tiny annex of Satan's kingdom.

"I know it's a bit cramped." Suze shrugged. "This is usually a double, apparently, but they had to force a triple due to budget issues. I hope you don't mind that I took the built-in shelving over my bed."

I looked. It was less space than my closet half. "Don't mind at all," I answered truthfully.

"Libby couldn't have fit all her really important things like *shoes* in there," Ashling remarked snidely, still gazing at her Susannah Fennyweather portraiture.

"Why don't I show you around?" Suze suggested.

"Please," I said gratefully.

We stepped over the threshold from one set of warped wooden floorboards to another. Once upon a time, it must have been a beautiful house. Now, however, it could have used a bit of work. The paint was peeling on the whitewashed wooden clapboards outside, and the floor was so uneven you had to watch your step to avoid face-planting.

"Do you know when the house was built, Suze?" I asked. "It looks sort of Greek Revival—1830s?"

"Good eye," she said approvingly. "It was built in 1833 by Josiah Helms, a prosperous local merchant, and, like you said, neoclassically inspired."

The Greek Revival is really cool. Dev would probably say *cool* is a relative term here, but whatever. Following archaeological discoveries in the eighteenth century, ancient Greece suddenly became awesome—just like a couple of years ago when everybody started wearing leggings and decided the '80s were back, you know? All these archaeologists-architects came back from seeing Greece and started building things in the classical tradition, but with a new twist (neoclassical, get it?), and soon everybody wanted in. In America Thomas Jefferson pushed it big time—which is why so many of the buildings in D.C. look like Greek temples. Because the Greeks had basically invented democracy, Americans saw themselves as Ancient Greece, Part Two, once America broke away from England to become a democratic country. Greek Revival architecture became a symbol of the new democracy, of national pride—a uniting force for our brand-new country. That Thomas Jefferson was no fool. Plus, he was a super-sassy redhead.

We passed through the skinny hallway into the living room. There was a large, sagging striped couch sprouting stuffing, a lopsided bookshelf, and an ancient TV.

"Believe it or not, we get cable," Suze said, pointing to the TV.

"That is hard to believe." It looked like the last thing that TV had broadcast was the moon landing.

I walked over to examine the room's sole decorative object: an oil painting of an ancient, rain-soaked mariner at the helm of a schooner. He was dressed like the guy on the fish sticks box but had the general demeanor of Captain Ahab. I had never seen an oil painting look quite so pissed off.

"The 'library' is something else too," Suze added.

I bent down to look in the crooked book shelves under Captain Ahab. Seven different maritime histories, *Knotcraft: The Practical and Entertaining Art of Knot Tying*, an illustrated children's version of the collected works of Robert Louis Stevenson, *Joy of Cooking*, a handful of romance novels boasting shirtless Fabios, *Betty Crocker Cookie Book,* and *Horton Hears a Who!.*

"So . . . lots of summer fun tying knots and baking cookies?"

Suze shook her head. "I wouldn't bet on the cookies. Check out the kitchen."

I followed her through the open door frame, narrowly avoiding a piece of hanging lintel. The kitchen was filthy and beyond cluttered with the oddest assortment of kitchen appliances I'd ever seen. There was a crepe pan, six soufflé ramekins, and an apple peeler, yet no spoons. Mysterious bottles and boxes of nonperishable food items spilled out of the cabinets, over the counters, and onto the oven. A few alphabet magnets decorated the once white refrigerator.

The kitchen was already occupied, by a boy sitting at the hefty wooden table with a bag of radishes and a tub of hummus. I was seriously beginning to think I'd passed Rod Serling somewhere and had now entered the Twilight Zone. You think you know what tall is, until you see a six-foot-seven gangly teenager with a huge 'fro unfold himself from a kitchen chair.

"I'm Neil." He extended the longest arm I'd ever seen to shake my hand. "I'm here to film a documentary on the last living lighthouse keepers. And to abuse my unlimited kayaking privileges."

"Cool." I smiled.

"Neil lives upstairs, with two marine biologists," Suze explained.

"What are you here for?" he asked.

"I'm the Education and Interpretation intern."

"She's not real Interpretation!" Ashling yelled from the other room.

"The walls have ears," Suze whispered fearfully, darting paranoid glances around the room.

"She's just a camp counselor!" Ashling yelled again.

"Technically true." I gritted my teeth. "I'm in charge of Girls of Long Ago Camp."

"Nothing wrong with camp counseling." Neil nodded, Adam's apple bobbing. "What's Girls of Long Ago Camp?"

"Eight- to ten-year-old girls learn open-hearth cooking, needlework, soap making, candle making, spinning . . . domestic arts. Basically they do all the things eight- to ten-year-old girls would have done two centuries ago, give or take," I explained.

"You know how to do that stuff?" he asked, reaching back to dip a radish in the hummus and pop it in his mouth. It crunched loudly.

"Some of it." I shrugged. "The rest, they're gonna train me, supposedly. I mean, my favorite area is American social history, specifically women's studies, so I know what it all is, in theory. Hopefully the practical application shouldn't be too hard."

"I don't have to bother with practical application." Suze grinned. "That's why I'm a research librarian. I'll be up to my ears in all the maritime folklore a girl could wish for," she finished dreamily.

"Radish, ladies?" Neil polished off another one.

"Umm, no thanks," I demurred. "I should finish unpacking. But it was really nice to meet you." Odd snack choices aside, he seemed nice enough.

"You too. The marine biologists are out collecting samples, but I'm sure you'll meet them later."

"Right." Suze and I nodded and headed out, leaving Neil to his radishes.

"It's gonna be weird, living with a boy," she whispered as we left the kitchen. "Having him around all day."

"Oh, I don't know, he'll be upstairs. It probably won't be that weird," I mused.

"I've been at the same all-girls school since kindergarten," she confided. "This may already be the most time I've ever spent with a guy our age."

"Yikes," I blurted out, without thinking. "Oh my God." I blushed. "I didn't mean that! I'm so sorry, I wasn't thinking; it just sort of popped out . . ."

"It's okay." She laughed. "Unusual, I know. I'm like the last unicorn."

"I'm leaving for orientation," Ashling yelled. "NOW!"

"Keep your pants on," I said. "We should probably go with her, right?" I asked Suze.

She nodded.

"Oookay." I sighed reluctantly. "Let me just get my sunglasses."

Ashling was clipping on a fanny pack in the bedroom as I pulled a pair of giant white sunglasses out of the purse I'd left on my bed.

"You're wearing . . . that?" Ashling asked.

"Um . . . yes?" I hadn't meant for it to come out like a question, but it did. I had planned a special nautically inspired outfit for my first day—an adorable seersucker strapless button-down top, cuffed-hem linen shorts, striped canvas ballet flats, and the pièce de résistance, a silver anchor necklace.

"Hoo boy." Ashling huffed. Clearly, I had made a sartorial error in her expert eyes. I wondered idly if she would have outright strangled me with said silver necklace if I'd gone with my original plan and worn espadrilles. Ashling stormed out, Suze and I following in her wake.

The screen door slammed shut, wobbled on its hinges for a moment, but somehow managed to stay in the door frame, seemingly only through sheer force of will. It was a beautiful day, and the heat hit me like a tangible force as we stepped out into the sunshine.

"It's humid here, isn't it?" My curly hair was rapidly expanding into Afro-tastic proportions. I tried to pat it down, but that only made it redouble its efforts to defy gravity.

"You look like a lion."

"Thanks, Ashling."

Ashling criticizing my hair was kind of like Jenna Jameson condemning premarital sex. Suze shook her close-cropped head, warning me not to start anything. We plodded down the sidewalk.

"The museum is this way, the way we're going, and the beach and downtown area are in the other direction," Ashling explained like a bored tour guide. "You exit the house, walk for five minutes either left or right, and you hit a destination. *Anyone*"—she looked at me—"should be able to figure that out."

"*Mmm.*" I nodded. *What* was going on here? I had never met someone who disliked me so much, so quickly! I mean, I don't want to sound stuck-up, but usually people like me! I had always gotten "plays well with others" on my report card back at Eunice Norton Elementary. I had thought that I was just not an interpersonal-conflict kind of girl. But right now it looked like this was shaping up to be an interpersonal conflict on the level of Batman and the Joker.

Luckily, it really was only five minutes—five awkward, silent minutes, but five minutes nonetheless. We had reached the rambling white farmhouse that served as the administrative headquarters of Camden Harbor: the Museum of Maine and the Sea. Located just outside the gates of the living history museum, it held all the staff offices. I'd been here just this morning to pick up a key to my less-than-luxurious accommodations.

Ashling pushed open the door and marched straight up to the receptionist's desk. "We're the interns," she announced proudly.

"How nice, dear." The receptionist, a round, motherly woman smiled. "Head down the hallway and wait in the Oak Room—last door on your left. Maddie will be there in just a minute. We're just dealing with something right now."

They must have been dealing with something big—I could hear indeterminate yelling noises floating from one of the endless rooms off the hall. The Oak Room was just like the rest —dark wood, burgundy carpet, heavy floral drapes, brimming bookshelves, and stern nineteenth-century New Englanders frowning down from oil paintings. We took seats in three of the Quaker-style chairs around the oval table that dominated the room. The yelling drifted in from the next room over, louder, and now I could make out what they were saying:

"Maddie, I need you on my side on this one," a man's voice pleaded.

"I don't know," a woman said, hedging. "It was just some kid. It might be nothing."

"This isn't the first sighting and you know it," he argued back heatedly. "There've been enough sightings that it's definitely something. This is happening, Maddie, whether you want it to or not. So we might as well do something about it! Do you have any idea how much business this could bring in?"

"President Harrow doesn't want to capitalize on any of this ghost stuff. He thinks it's cheap—"

"And it's a museum, not a tourist trap, blah, blah, blah. I've heard it all before," he interrupted. "But we're in serious financial trouble, Maddie. We're at an all-time attendance low, and this place is hemorrhaging money. Wouldn't anything—*anything*—be worth it to get more people in? Especially just a silly little ghost story? What's the harm in that?"

"I'll have to think about it, Roger." She sighed. "If people see this 'ghost' again and it starts to really become something, I'll think about it, okay?"

"It already is something, Maddie, four sightings. It—"

"I'll think about it, Roger," she said, finishing the conversation. "I have to go welcome the interns."

A door slammed, and a pair of heels clicked down the corridors. Not a moment later, a harried-looking thirty-something in a slim-flitting black pantsuit pushed open the door.

"Hi," she said breathlessly. "Sorry about that. Thanks for waiting. I'm Maddie. The education director and internship coordinator." She had the kind of red hair usually considered striking on women and unattractive on men. It suited her. She twisted it into a low bun at the nape of her neck as she took a seat at the head of the table. "Welcome to Camden Harbor, the Museum of Maine and the Sea." She smiled. "In here, it's always 1791." We smiled and nodded in return. "Brief introduction, then down to business. So, as I'm sure you guys all know from the brochure we sent you, this area—called Mengunticook, or 'great swells of the sea,' by the Penobscot Abenaki Indians—was settled just after the conclusion of the French and Indian War. The settlement served as an American encampment during the Revolution and was incorporated as the town of Camden Harbor in 1791. Which is why, when the museum was built in the late 1920s, the founders decided to recreate Camden Harbor as it would have been at the time of its incorporation. Although not a brick-for-brick reproduction, the Camden Harbor buildings give visitors the experience of what life would have been like in a small New England fishing village of the period. I'm sure this isn't new information." We nodded again. "Great. I'm just gonna give you guys a quick spiel about scheduling, what your days will be like here, that kind of thing . . . Really quick, I promise, and we'll be on our way. We're big into on-the-job learning here."

Suze and I exchanged nervous glances. Maddie pulled out a folder from the attaché case she'd brought in with her. "All righty, let's see." She flipped it open. "Ashling."

"Yes, ma'am." Ashling pulled a minuscule notebook and pen out of her fanny pack. "Before you begin, I already know what I'm doing. I am extremely experienced in first-person interpretation, and I was planning to proceed with my current character."

"Okay." Maddie tried to smile politely. "Well, that's great. So you'll be walking around the harbor, in character, interacting with guests all day, in a freeform environment."

"That is correct," Ashling confirmed, like she was the boss.

"Then I guess all we need to do is get you a fitting. Suze?" She moved on. Suze waved. "When we next meet up, for your training session, I'll take you over to the Research Library, where you'll be assisting the head librarian and the curator with whatever they're working on, as well as researching a project of your own choosing."

"Great." Suze nodded happily.

"So that makes you Libby." Maddie turned to me. "Girls of Long Ago Camp starts on Monday. In the mornings, you and the girls will do hearth cooking, and then in the afternoons, different craft projects. You can schedule needlework, knitting, quilting, flower pressing, all of that, at your discretion. They'll go over it in more detail at your domestic arts training this weekend and show you where all the supplies are, so you can make some kind of lesson plan." She pursed her lips.

"Awesome." I smiled.

"Great." Maddie closed the folder. "Glad this is going so well. We'll be off to the costume shack in no time. Ashling and Libby, you'll be in period dress, but whenever you're not, you'll join Suze in wearing the official Camden Harbor uniform: a blue polo with the Camden Harbor logo." She pulled one seemingly out of thin air and held it up. It wasn't particularly cute—a generic royal blue polo with a white schooner and "Camden Harbor: The Museum of Maine and the Sea" embroidered above the left breast pocket. "And then," she continued, "your own khaki bottoms. Shorts, pants, what have you."

"Wait, wait, wait." I raised my hand. "Nobody mentioned a uniform. We have to wear that all the time?"

"Malibu Barbie is worried she won't be able to show off the wardrobe from the dream house," Ashling muttered.

"Malibu? Malibu?! I'm from *Minnesota*," I hissed back.

"Yes, all the time," Maddie confirmed. "When you're not in costume. And when you are in costume, no makeup."

"N-no makeup?" I stuttered. "Um, I don't mean to be a pain in the butt about this, but I'm blond—"

"We are well aware," Ashling deadpanned.

"What I meant," I continued, "is that I look really weird without eye makeup. Like an alien. Because I have blond eyelashes? It might, um, scare the kids . . ." I trailed off.

"As a redhead, I am familiar with the phenomenon," Maddie said dryly.

"No, but *seriously*," I stressed. "You're underestimating the gravity of the situation. Once I left for school without eye makeup and everyone thought I was sick and my friend Dev tried to send me to the nurse for a mono test, but it was just because I overslept and didn't have time to put on any eyeliner—"

"We appreciate the enormity of your sacrifice." Maddie held up her hand for silence and cut me off. "But no makeup."

Ashling rolled her eyes and smiled smugly.

"And finally, obviously, whenever you're in costume, no cell phones."

"NO CELL PHONES?!" I exploded.

"They shatter the illusion of the eighteenth-century village," Maddie explained calmly.

"But what if we hide them from the tourists? And only check them when no one's around?" I wheedled. What if Dev needed to call me? What if Meryl Streep needed him to get an unpublished Harry Potter manuscript and I was the only one who could help? Not that I'd know how to do that anyway, but that was beside the point.

"Nope." Maddie stood firm.

"Come on, Suze, back me up here," I whispered. Sure, Suze seemed a little repressed, maybe, but I was holding out a hope that she was a normal human.

"Sorry, Libby." She shook her head. "I work in a library. We're not exactly pro-phone."

"Oh, fine," I grumbled. I'd find a way. I was resourceful. Like a pioneer woman.

"Now that that's settled"—Maddie picked up her attaché case—"let's get you gals fitted."

We filed out of the Oak Room, left the administrative farmhouse, and went through the staff entrance to Camden Harbor, which was a swinging gate in a white picket fence behind a butter-yellow house.

"This is the Bromleigh Homestead." Maddie pointed to the house as we wound our way through the garden. "It's where you'll be, Libby. This is where Girls of Long Ago Camp is."

It was a beautiful house, older than the one we lived in but perfectly restored. It was right on the main road, a gravel path ringed with clapboard houses surrounding a green and facing the harbor. Three-masted tall ships bobbed gently in the sea. The whole place looked like a postcard; like an idyllic dream of New England. And maybe it wasn't totally real, but it was real enough: I was here.

"The costume shack is that tiny white house on the other side of the town green, down by the quay, next to the cooper's shop." Maddie indicated a small building in the distance. "Let's cut across the green."

And, wow, as we got closer, I had never wanted to take a shortcut more in my life. It looked like an entire Harlequin Historical series had escaped the romance shelves at Barnes & Noble. Fifteen of the tannest, hottest guys I'd ever seen in my life were running around the green in open-necked white shirts and tight tan breeches, tossing something leather that looked like an early football and shaking their sun-bleached locks.

Now, here is the dirty little secret of almost every girl who loves history: somewhere along the line, she fell for a fictional historical hottie. Maybe it was Colin Firth as Mr. Darcy in that dripping wet shirt. Or Clark Gable imagining Vivien Leigh without her shimmy. Or a rascally Hugh Grant charming a girl *Sense*less. Even Leonardo DiCaprio clinging to the *Titanic* as he slowly turned blue. Believe you me. If a girl loves history, this probably happened. Many of us dream of a time of true love, courtly manners, and real gentlemen. A world away from varsity hockey players chugging PBR post-game in the parking lot and what my mom had once mistakenly referred to as "friends with privileges," which I privately thought of as the surest sign of the romantic apocalypse.

Dev blamed my perpetual singlehood on this problem. He told me I needed to stop waiting for a poem and accept a proposition, because Mr. Darcy just didn't exist. Boy, was Dev wrong—it was like a Mr. Darcy/sexy pirate hybrid convention out here. Mr. Darcy *was* real. I'd just been looking in the wrong place.

I was staring, slack jawed, at the 1790s *Playgirl* spread in front of me. "Who," I said, gasping, "are they?"

"Squaddies." She nodded brusquely. "Stay away."

"What, er, who are Squaddies?" I noticed Suze next to me. She appeared to have frozen completely and stopped functioning altogether.

"Demo Squad," she explained. "Schooner Demonstration. They work on the ships."

"Oh," I said, drooling, "climbing all that rigging must really define your arms."

"Yes." Maddie eyed me warily. "Like I said, stay away from the Squaddies. They're trouble. You especially, Libby. Be careful."

"Wha—what?" I snapped out of my trance. "Why me especially?"

"Because they send Squaddies to chop wood for open-hearth cooking. For you."

"Dooooo they." I smiled slowly. How nice. How nice for me.

The ball went long, and the cutest Squaddie broke away from the pack to chase it. He caught it neatly, skidding to a stop mere feet away. A thick, straight shock of sandy blond hair fell across gray-blue eyes as he smiled right at me, displaying blindingly white teeth. My heart stopped.

"Move along, Squaddie," Maddie ordered.

He shrugged and jogged off to join the rest of the Hottie Patrol, turning over his shoulder to look at me again and smile. Once Maddie's back was turned, he waved. Ashling be damned. I thanked all my lucky stars that I had gone strapless.

"Heh," Suze said in a strangled little voice as we continued across the green.

"I know!" I sighed rapturously in return.

"Disgusting," Ashling muttered. I didn't know what planet she was from. That boy may have been many things, but "disgusting" was not one of them. I floated six inches off the ground the rest of the way to the costume shack.

After reminding us to show up promptly at nine for training the following morning, Maddie hurried off to the education offices to coordinate some last-minute camp details. The costume shack really was a shack. The stout older woman ruling the domain pulled Suze back into an area so crammed with clothes, you could hardly see the door, leaving me and Ashling in a waiting area containing one folding metal chair and a *Camden Crier* from February '02. Ashling took the chair. I picked up what I gathered was the local newspaper.

A few minutes later Suze was done, and the costume lady pulled Ashling back into her lair. I flipped through the *Crier*, skimming an article about the school board fudging standardized testing results. Fifteen minutes of flipping later, Ashling returned and it was my turn.

Within, it was even more stuffed with clothes than I'd thought.

"First things first." The lady tossed a polo shirt at me. "Here."

I held it up. It was enormous. "Do you, um, have a small?"

"That is the small."

"Fan-tastic." Now I had an attractive shirtdress. Okay, that's a lie—I had a shirtdress.

"Let's get you kitted up." The costume lady started bustling around, simultaneously stripping me and collecting garments: wool stockings that tied above my knees; a loose-fitting shift, which looked like a linen nightgown; a not-so-loose set of stays, which was like a pointy-ended tube top with boning and made my torso look like an ice cream cone with two scoops on top; and three different petticoats. I had on more clothes in my underwear in the eighteenth century than I did fully dressed in the twenty-first.

I took an experimental breath. My lungs pushed against the stiff boning of the stays, but I could breathe. Sort of. I was actually lucky, because for American women, late eighteenth-century stays were more like bras than nineteenth-century corsets — their primary purpose was support, not waist minimization. Stays encouraged good posture (definitely no slouching in my future), and supported and lifted the bosom. And my stays were succeeding a bit too well on that front. With each breath, I was half afraid my boobs would just break free — because the stays were flattening out my torso, my boobs had nowhere to go but up. And up they went. I tugged my shift to make sure it was extra secure.

"And the dress . . . How's this?" She held up what looked like a brown burlap sack.

"Do you have anything a little more . . . saucy?" Saucy enough to seduce a Squaddie, maybe.

"I'll . . . check." She raised an eyebrow. "Honey, you know you're gonna be scrubbing pots, not doing the minuet."

"I know," I agreed, "but they're just so beautiful." I looked longingly at the rows of dresses above my head.

That did the trick. I'd somehow flipped a switch and turned her from a troll into my new best friend. "Let me rustle up some options." She beamed.

She returned with a linsey-woolsey sapphire-blue day dress,

PILGRIMS DON'T WEAR PINK

another in striped sky-blue poplin, and my favorite, a pink confection with little white flowers that had an underskirt in contrasting colors that peeked through. I clapped in delight.

"I love them!" I squealed. "Thank you, thank you, thank you!"

"You are so very welcome, dear," she replied. "If you want, even though we're not supposed to do this, you can come in anytime and switch them out for new ones." She winked conspiratorially.

"No!" I gasped in joyous disbelief.

"Shhh!" She shushed me merrily. "Now, you'll want to keep these in the linen press upstairs at the Bromleigh Homestead. Wear your Camden Harbor uniform over in the mornings and change in the homestead. The dresses will be waiting in the linen press for you tomorrow morning."

"Got it."

Tomorrow was looking better and better. I whistled as I made my way home from the costume shack. I knew, once back at the house, I had to face two of my least favorite things: unpacking and dealing with Ashling. Both of these activities required my full attention, so at the end of an evening full of both, I was more than happy to collapse into bed and read. I hadn't brought that many books, which after seeing the "library" in the living room, I was beginning to think was a fatal error. I picked up my well-read copy of *Northanger Abbey,* happily turning its familiar pages. I'd always thought Henry Tilney was one of Austen's most underappreciated heroes. So witty and intelligent and funny, and he and Catherine are so perfect for each other, and—

"I go to sleep at ten," Ashling said, then abruptly turned out the lights, plunging the room into darkness.

"Actually, um, I was gonna read for a bit, and—"

"Good night."

Well, if nothing else, come August—if I survived—I'd sure be well rested.

chapter two

I really was wearing pants, but no one believed me. On the walk to the museum grounds, four cars rolled down their windows to whistle, two different mothers covered their sons' eyes, and Ashling kept huffing something that sounded suspiciously like "skank." I really wasn't pantsless. I only looked like it. My standard-issue blue polo shirt just happened to be longer than the only pair of khaki shorts I owned. Ah, the perils of being short.

I had never thought I'd be so relieved to don something that reached down to my ankles, but after my pants-free walk of shame, I wriggled gratefully into my layers of petticoats and the blue linsey-woolsey dress. There was an apron in there too, which I tied on — who knew how messy things were going to get.

Downstairs, a capable-looking woman in her early sixties was waiting for me in the kitchen. She looked like she could help a cow give birth. Or had maybe worked as a park ranger.

"I'm Ruth," she said as she grasped my hand firmly. "We've got a lot of work to do, kid."

Ruth wasn't kidding. Back before kitchen stoves became widespread in the nineteenth century, Americans cooked on an open hearth, either hanging things above the flames to roast or heating things by burying them in the warmth of the ashes. The one here looked a bit like something out of a brick-oven pizza restaurant. We swept the ashes into the center of the hearth and built up the fire using wood stacked by the back door. Ruth selected different cast-iron pots, nestling two lidded ones into the ashes, hanging another from one of many hooks dangling above the fire, and setting a frying pan on a trivet. All of the pots were ridiculously heavy and left midnight black streaks on my hands. As the fire heated up, Ruth led me down a narrow staircase into the cellar.

"No one comes down here but you. You hear? No one," she said seriously. "This"—she gestured to a refrigerator—"is the only modern appliance in the house. Here's where you'll get all the cooking supplies that don't come from the garden and aren't upstairs in jars, like flour, sugar, molasses, et cetera."

And those supplies turned out to be . . . lard. Ruth opened the refrigerator to reveal a solid wall of boxed snow-capped lard. More lard than I had thought existed in the continental United States.

"Eggs are on the side"—she flipped open the egg holder —"and milk is on the bottom inside the door. All the meat's in the freezer." She closed the refrigerator door and opened the freezer on top, which was packed with freezer-burned bloody carcasses. It looked like someone had hacked up a human corpse and stashed the evidence. I tried not to gag.

"You ever rendered pork fat before?"

"N-no," I stammered.

"First time for everything."

Ruth loaded my arms with a frozen roast and a lifetime supply of lard, and we headed upstairs. Lard, it turns out, is not so gross. It's really not that different from butter. Raw meat, however . . . like really raw meat—drawing in horseflies from the barn, dripping globules of yellow fat onto the counter as it defrosts—is another story. I stopped breathing through my nose as I hacked up Babe the pig and transferred him to the frying pan under Ruth's watchful eye. It bubbled merrily away in a sea of lard, as I seriously considered a vegan lifestyle.

It got better once I'd conquered the beast. Ruth took me out back to show me around the kitchen garden. In addition to the flowers there for purely decorative purposes, there was an herb patch, a vegetable section dominated almost entirely by beets, some sprawling blueberry bushes, and a mostly empty apple barrel. Except for the little signs indicating what was what for the visitors, it was exactly like what a colonial woman would have had for everyday use. We headed back in to steam some beet greens in one cast-iron pot and boil the beets in another. Looking at my hands stained red with beet juice, an idea occurred to me . . . hmm. When Ruth wasn't looking, I used a pewter plate as a mirror and blended some beet juice into my cheeks as impromptu blush. Not bad! I rubbed some on my lips. It actually looked like a shade of Burt's Bees lip-gloss I'd lost last summer. I wasn't going to break the modern makeup rule, and I certainly wasn't going to crush beetles into red lip stain like actual colonial women had done in the pre-Revlon era, but in the immortal words of Tim Gunn on *Project Runway*, I was going to make it work. I swiped some soot from the top of the bread oven (we weren't using it) and streaked it on my eyelids. Easy, breezy, beautiful, ColonialGirl.

Baking I actually have a bit of a knack for. Last year I took first place at the Minnesota State Fair Bake-Off with my caramel apple pie recipe. I practically learned to read on my mom's *Martha Stewart Living* magazines. Martha may not be super into lard and molasses, but I think even she would have been impressed with the perfectly steamed Indian pudding I produced an hour later. Ruth explained that open-hearth baking was like using a Dutch oven when you go camping. I don't camp, so this analogy was lost on me. But it wasn't so bad. You stuck your baked good in a cast-iron lidded pot, put the pot in the ashes, and used a pair of tongs to give the pot a quarter turn every fifteen minutes, to ensure it baked evenly. It was a lot riskier and less precise than modern baking, because if you opened the lid to check on it, you put the whole enterprise in jeopardy. Plus, back then cookbooks weren't widely used. No Martha giving you step-by-step instructions on how to blanch your marcona almonds or create aromatic herb bundles for parchment-baked perch. Thankfully, the homestead had its own special book of handwritten recipes on the shelf in between the jar of Brer Rabbit Molasses and a honey pot that functioned largely as a bee cemetery.

By the end of the day, I had fashioned a feast of pork fat, beet greens, and Indian pudding, none of which I was remotely interested in eating. I was sweaty, sooty, smelly, and my arms ached from lugging around those insanely heavy pots. Tired and gross as I was, it was actually strangely satisfying. Sure, I'd only produced four tons of pork-infused lard, but I felt like I'd really accomplished something. More so than, say, writing a five-paragraph essay. Or nailing the smoky-eye look.

Ruth sent me out back to scrub the pots under the water pump. The lard was . . . crusty. As I pumped water and rubbed my hands raw trying to get out globs of stuck-on pork fat, contemplating the irony that the tallow soap I was using was also made out of animal fat, I fought down the urge to vomit for the millionth time that day. I was surrounded by animal fat. Even the cleaning products felt dirty! Greasy, gritty water soaked the hem of my skirts and little black cast-iron flecks came loose, settling in my clothes, my hair, my everywhere. Suddenly, I had a flash of the cute, clean girl who'd arrived in her canvas ballet flats, innocent, naive, and a stranger to lard. It was all just too much. I put down the last of the mostly clean pots.

So, yes, I'll admit it, I'd broken the cell phone rule. I'd stuck it in my bra before I left the house to smuggle it into the museum. We were allowed to wear modern underwear under our costumes, but I had a horrible feeling that Ashling was going full-on commando in the name of historical accuracy. Not me —I love history, but I love personal hygiene more. I like a little something on under my petticoats, thank you very much. So I had a pink lacy bra that doubled as a stealth cell phone holder under my stays. I know, it was bad that I'd brought the phone. But I'd thought that Dev might have needed me. Turned out, I needed him. I looked around—Ruth was busy in the house, and none of the museum visitors on the road could see around to the garden, but . . . Bingo! I spied the almost-empty apple barrel. Perfect cover. I leaned over, stuck my head in the barrel, pulled the phone out of my boobs, and dialed.

"Dev!" I sobbed. "I smell like a slaughterhouse!"

"What? Hello?" he answered, confused. "Who is this? If this is PETA again, I don't know how you got this number, but back off. We are running the 'Fun Fur' piece, and there's nothing you can do about it."

"What? No! It's not PETA—it's Libby."

"Libby? Why would you smell like a slaughterhouse? Aren't you wearing your Burberry Brit?" It was hard to hear him.

"Nobody ever mentioned how much lard was involved in the good old days." I sniffled.

"You did not just say 'lard' to me." Static. "I'm on a no-fat, no-carb diet. Don't even think 'lard' in my general direction."

"Where are you?" I asked. "There's a lot of background noise."

"Starbucks," Dev replied briskly. "I'm trying to construct a carry-able tower out of four nonfat half-caf lattes, two Cinnamon Dolce Light Frappuccinos, three shots of espresso, and a reduced-fat strawberry scone, and it is *not* going well." Shuffling noises. "How are things with you? Aside from the L-word. How're the other nerds?"

"They hate me," I moaned miserably. "It's like *Legally Blonde.*"

"Really?" he asked. "That's weird. You're not even that blond. You use the honey-to-caramel shade of Sheer Blonde shampoo."

"I know," I whined, "but they're treating me like Elle Woods's sluttier, stupider younger sister." Okay, fine, really it was only one of them, but I was in a self-pitying mood and felt like the whole world was out to get me. And I wanted to whine.

"You? Really. Really? You have way too many freckles and sometimes your hair frizzes. I mean you're cute, but you're no Reese Witherspoon . . ."

"Exactly!"

"I mean, they should have *seen* you when I first met you in that tragic pink turtleneck you thought was so chic."

"It *was* chic three years ago!" I protested.

"You were a well-meaning mess. I made you what you are!"

"I'd be offended, if I didn't sort of agree. They're totally misjudging me. I'm not a dumb blonde! I'm just a dork who likes shoes."

"Too true," he agreed, a little more readily than I was comfortable with. "Well," he asked, amid more rustling sounds, "is there anything good in the Clamhole?"

A tall, blond, muscular thought drifted through my brain. I smiled.

"I may have hit the man jackpot."

"Explain, Miss Libby."

"Sexy sailors!" I squealed. "In knickers!"

"Shut up!"

"True!" I giggled. "But probably nowhere near as sexy as all the models you're seeing, right?"

"They don't let me near the models," he said sadly.

"Well . . . did you meet Anne Hathaway yet?"

"Libby"—he paused dramatically—"I . . . AM . . . Anne Hathaway!"

"Um, excuse me?" Someone from the outside addressed me. Startled, I lost my balance and shifted forward, toppling into the apple barrel. All except for my legs, that is, which were kicking in the open air.

"Eeek!"

"Libby? Libby?!" Dev shrieked amid a great deal of static. Outside the barrel, I could hear a guy laughing. Uproariously.

"Dev, I'll call you back." I shut the phone.

That idiot outside the barrel was still howling. He was laughing so hard, I think I heard a few snorts.

"Um, a little help here!" I yelled. "Please!"

Finally, still chuckling, whoever it was came over to the barrel, grabbed my waist, and lifted me out of it, planting me back on solid ground.

"You know," my Johnny-come-lately rescuer said, removing a pair of rectangular plastic-framed glasses to wipe tears of laughter from his eyes, "I don't think they wore underwear in the 1790s. Definitely not Hello Kitty underwear." He dissolved into giggles again. And yes, I was right—those were snorts. He was laughing like Miss Piggy on acid or something.

My cheeks flamed. "Thanks for the history lesson. Were you going to just leave me in the barrel for your own personal amusement?"

"If I didn't have somewhere to be, yeah, I would've left you in there longer," he said, chuckling. "It was pretty funny."

This stupid, tall, scruffy, brown-eyed boy may have had Clark Kent's glasses, but he had none of his heroic impulses. Or manners. Or classic good looks.

"It was *not* funny," I snapped. I pulled a disturbingly mushy piece of apple out of my hair and violently threw it to the ground. Oh, gross, gross, gross.

Having composed himself, he put his glasses back on, blinking rapidly. "I should be hearing the dulcet chime of a thank-you right about . . . now."

"Th-th-thank you?!" I nearly choked on it.

"You're welcome."

"No, no, I wasn't thanking you!" I protested. "That was an expression of disbelief! Why on earth would I thank you?!"

"It is customary in these situations." He straightened his glasses, blinking again. Oh my God. He was totally one of those guys who spent all his free time playing World of War-craft, blinking at his computer screen, and being all "It is cus-tomary in these situations for Orcs to cede to humans when invoking the wrath of the Lich King" or something equally gross. You could just tell. He had WoW computer nerd written all over him. There was a whole troupe of them at SPA. They spent their lunches and free periods holed up in the computer lab, emerging only to go to class or to rush home at the end of the day to play some more.

I looked him up and down, from the top of his curly brown hair to his "My Other Car Is the Millennium Falcon" ringer tee to his fraying cargo shorts and beat-up black Converses — whoa, extra tragic. I mean, seriously, it was like a mountain climber and an IT guy had a baby and decided to raise it in Vermont with the help of a Phish-loving nanny. Someone who dressed so badly wasn't even worth a telling-off. Clearly, he was so socially hopeless (hello, *Star Wars* T-shirt) that anything in-volving manners or basic human interaction was just beyond him. So I said, with all the dignity I could muster, streaked with soot and bedaubed with apple mush: "You, sir, are a butt-face. Thanks for nothing."

I spun on my heel and marched back into the house.

"Wait!" he called after me. "Hey, Hello Kitty! Come back!"

I latched the door shut. Buttface? Yikes. Not my finest comeback. But whatever, he wasn't worth anything better. I mean, eeuw, the way he was snottily prompting *me* to say thank you? Like *I* needed the manners lecture? After he just left me there to laugh at?! And what was with those stupid glasses, anyway? What, were they supposed to be ironic or something? I stomped back into the kitchen.

"All cleaned up?" Ruth asked. I nodded. "Good." I swept the hearth into a neat pile of ashes, and we went into the parlor.

"This is where you and the girls will do the crafts. It said on your résumé you have knitting and needlepoint experience?"

I nodded. I am a girl of odd and diverse talents with little to no practical value.

"Then you know what to do. We should have everything you need."

And they did. I could have run an underground craft supply store out of that parlor, doing a roaring trade in black-market yarns and embroidery floss. As Ruth opened cabinets, showing me where they kept knitting needles, embroidery hoops, and even a flower press, she made nonbusiness conversation for the first time. I suspect she was inspired because there was no longer any danger of either of us being scalded by a vat of hot, bubbling lard, which, incidentally, crackles and pops, like Rice Krispies but gross.

"So," Ruth asked mischievously, "have you seen the ghost yet?"

"No, I only got here yesterday." I arranged balls of yarn in a big wicker basket by the window. "What ghost?"

"You haven't heard about it?"

"Um, sort of." I didn't think a half-overheard yelling match between the internship coordinator and some guy named Roger really counted as hearing about it.

"Ahh." She nodded. "You see the schooner closest to us out there in the harbor? The little one? She's called the *Lettie Mae Howell.*"

"Yep." I peered out the window, smushing my nose against

the thick pane. It left a soot print. I quickly wiped it off with a clean patch on my elbow.

"There have now been four separate sightings of a man in early American clothing, a silent sailor, a ghostly figure all in white."

"Spooky."

"He appears only after dark, then vanishes. The *Lettie Mae* was originally named something else—the *Sachem* or something like that. She was shipwrecked off the coast of Cape Cod in 1804, and nearly the entire crew drowned. This ghost sailor is supposed to be one of them. Anyway, some dunderheaded merchant rebuilt the ship and renamed her after his wife. And anybody with half a brain knows renaming a ship is bad luck. Which is why this feller is back from the grave. Or so they say," she harrumphed. "Sounds like a lot of nonsense to me. Probably kids messing around."

"Probably," I agreed. Silently, though, I reasoned it was probably a creepy old lighthouse keeper in a glow-in-the-dark ghost mask. I'd watched a lot of *Scooby-Doo* as a kid. I knew how it worked. Actually . . . with gangly Neil's lighthouse-keeping expertise, Suze's Velma-librarian smarts, and my flair for accessories, we meddling kids were more than halfway toward forming a Scooby gang.

"I think you're ready for Monday." I realized Ruth was talking to me as I was wondering what I'd look like in a purple minidress and green scarf. Focus, Libby. "I'd start off with one of the simpler recipes and then play to your strengths with the crafts," Ruth advised.

"I was thinking I'd lead with needlepoint. Little sailboat

samplers embroidered in indigo thread." I could see them in my head—adorable. And accurate! Needlework was a really common pastime for colonial women, and homespun linen thread dyed with indigo was the most readily accessible material. Plus indigo is just beautiful. By the time I was done with this place, I would have Martha-ed Maine up!

"Good." Ruth nodded approvingly. "Good. They're usually a sweet group of girls, so you should have no problems. If the ghost doesn't get you, that is," she added.

I half expected her to punctuate it with a "Bah, humbug!"

"Clean yourself up, sweep the front steps, and you're done for the day. You did good, kid," she concluded gruffly.

Using the window's reflection, I wiped the sooty streaks off my forehead and repinned my hair out of my eyes. My beet-and-ash makeup line was holding up remarkably well, even hours later. Maybe I could market it as EverAsh EverLast. Grabbing a broom out of a tiny cupboard under the stairs, I headed out to the front steps. The sun was lower in the sky, just above the water, bathing everything in a golden glow. A whistled tune I recognized as "Hey, Ho, Blow the Man Down" drifted down the lane. It segued smoothly into a low wolfwhistle. The insanely hot Squaddie who had smiled at me yesterday was leaning against the front gate, in his tan breeches and white shirt, navy jacket flung casually over his shoulder.

"Some girls," he said with a rakish grin, "were just born to wear a corset." His eyes lingered on my neckline, and he whistled again.

So maybe he'd used a historically inaccurate term for eighteenth-century undergarments . . . and maybe on a modern street corner it would have been kind of pervy . . . but I felt like

I was in a movie. The star of my very own Ang Lee–directed period film or BBC-produced miniseries or historical HBO special. This, right now, was the life I had always wanted, but I was afraid only existed in my head or at the movies. Thrilled to the tips of my toes, I blushed to the roots of my hair.

"Your name, Cinderella?"

"Libby." If my life was a romance novel, sparks would have been flying and bosoms would have been heaving. But with a sailor dangling over the garden gate, for the first time I was entertaining the possibility that maybe life *was* a romance novel.

"Good." He plucked a primrose off the vine twining about the white picket fence. "Now I won't have to search the kingdom to find you again." He twirled the flower in between his fingers. "I'm Cameron." He squinted into the sun. "Cam."

"Cam." I sighed rapturously. I could hear an imaginary *West Side Story* orchestra tuning up: "The most beautiful sound I ever heard . . ." Except instead of "Maria," the violins were singing "Cameron."

"Come here often?" he joked.

"From now on? Every day." I grinned ruefully. "I work here now."

"Then now I know where I'll be." He tossed the rose up to the steps. I caught it as he quoted, "My bounty is as boundless as the sea, my love as deep."

"The more I give to thee, the more I have, for both are infinite," I completed the couplet. Thank you, freshman English.

Cam raised his eyebrows and let out a long, impressed whistle. "Until we meet again." He bowed, then bobbed his head toward the water. "I must down to the seas again." He slung his jacket over his shoulder and strolled confidently away, whistling "The Girl I Left Behind Me," which I recognized from a *Songs of Little House on the Prairie* tape I'd played until it fell apart when I was little. I watched him fade into the sunlight, wind ruffling his golden hair.

Primroses and poetry . . . I sighed and sniffed deeply. Sweet.

chapter three

If we were shooting *VH1: Camden Harbor,* this would not have qualified for Best Weekend Ever. In a series of unfortunate incidents including countless snide comments, the revoking of my TV privileges after the *Charm School* marathon I watched was deemed "lewd," and the theft of a strawberry-banana yogurt, the absolute low-light was when Ashling decided I was taking up more than my allotted one-third of the bathroom shelving. Consequently, she moved all of my toiletries into my bed, where I, unawares, rolled over them and ended up covered in shampoo. It wasn't as bad as pork fat, but it certainly wasn't pleasant. I couldn't wait to get out of the house for work on Monday. I practically skipped down the sidewalk and up the stairs of the Bromleigh Homestead. For the first day of camp, I donned the sky-blue striped poplin. The stripes were sort of nautical, and in case a certain totally romantic, Shakespeare-quoting, flower-tossing, chivalrous, charming, breathtakingly handsome Squaddie happened to pass by, the blue brought out my eyes. Once dressed, I walked over to the Welcome Center, where I'd be meeting my campers. On my way in, Maddie flagged me down.

"Hey." She hustled over, clipboard in hand. "Things are a little nuts. The first day of our busiest season, you know? Not that things are particularly busy this year," she muttered darkly. "Anyway." She shook her head to clear it. "You okay?"

"Yep."

"Good, good." She checked something off on the clip-board. "Camp ends at two, then I'll need you to head over to the administrative offices for an all-staff meeting–slash–press conference sort of deal."

"Press conference?" I asked, curious.

"Yes, press conference, the Oak Room, two fifteen. Attendance is mandatory. Over here!" she called, and waved at a blue polo-shirted employee, who was leading a group of ten little girls in old-fashioned dresses and pinafores. Clearly, they'd been to the costume shack too. "Over here!" she called again. The girls formed a group around us. "Miss Libby," she said, "these are your campers. Campers, this is Miss Libby. She's in charge now."

Maddie bustled off, frantically scratching at the clipboard with a chewed-up BIC pen.

"Hey, guys," I said as I gathered them in. "Let's hit the homestead. Follow me, and stick tightly together." The Welcome Center was really crowded, but I managed to shepherd my flock safely through. We chatted as we walked down the lane to the Bromleigh Homestead, and Ruth was right—they seemed like a sweet group of girls. Not that I was really surprised, because a historical domestic arts camp just doesn't seem like it would attract the wild ones. They squealed with delight and exclaimed over the house as I led them to the dining room, where I'd set up ten little calligraphy stations. I thought we'd start off by making colonial "nametags," using ink pots, parchment, and quill pens. About an hour and a million ink blots later, we finished. I punched holes in the tags and tied them around each girl's neck with a length of yarn. After a brief squabble over who got the purple yarn, we headed into the kitchen.

I had decided to follow Ruth's advice and keep it simple. No animal carcasses today. Or probably ever, if I had any say in the matter. Like Maddie had said, I was in charge now. And I was thinking we had a summer of baking ahead of us.

"Who likes lemonade?" I yelled.

"Me! Me! Me!" they shouted back.

"What about gingerbread?"

"Yay!"

The *yays* had it. Lemonade and gingerbread it was. The girls were enthusiastic but very respectful of the rules about the fire and the knives. I split them up into little teams, sending a few out to pump water, some to squeeze lemons, and others to measure sugar. Luckily, the water pump was hooked up to a modern, sanitized water source, so we didn't have to worry about bacteria. The lemonade came together quickly, and I turned my attention to the gingerbread. Flour flew like summer snow and covered us all in a light dusting. We made shapes in the flour on the table and powdered flour hearts onto our cheeks. Two of the girls carefully poured the batter into a tin pan, and I placed the pan into the Dutch oven in the ashes, explaining how the baking process worked while the rest looked on.

"Miss Libby! Miss Libby!" A tiny blonde with rainbow braces was peeking out the kitchen window. "There's a boy outside!" She giggled. "And he's not wearing a shirt!"

I quickly joined her at the window, and the rest of the girls swarmed around me. Cam was out in the backyard, chopping wood. And she was right—he wasn't wearing a shirt. Wow. Tacking the jib boom and hoisting the mainsail and whatever else they did must have been really, really good exercise. Sweat glistened on his tanned torso as the ax flashed in the sun. Now that the fire was really going, it was altogether too hot in that kitchen. I fanned myself futilely with a corner of my apron.

"He looks like a Disney prince," said one of the girls, giggling.

"He looks like John Smith from *Pocahontas*," another one corrected.

"Girls, let's get some lemonade, okay?" I suggested. I, for one, definitely needed to cool down. A couple of them followed me over to the earthenware pitcher, but most of the girls stayed clustered around the window. I pulled pewter mugs out at random and absent-mindedly poured several glasses. Never in a million years was Dev going to believe this. There was a sexy, shirtless lumberjack outside my window. I pinched myself. Nope, this time it wasn't a dream. I wondered if there was any way I could pull my illegal cell phone out of my bra and take a video to record this for posterity without being detected. Probably not.

"He's coming! Miss Libby, the boy is coming!" one of them shrieked, and the rest of the girls dispersed, echoing her shrieks, several running straight into my skirts. I pretended I was very busy and involved with a jar of molasses.

"Why, Miss Libby," Cam called, leaning over the kitchen door. It was one of those Dutch farmhouse doors that split in half, with the top half open and bottom half shut. "Oh, Miss Libby, Miss Libby," he called again, a twinkle in his eye. "Chopping all this wood is hot and thirsty work. You wouldn't have anything sweet and refreshing, now, would you?"

"We made lemonade," said a slip of a brunette peeping around from behind my skirts.

"Not quite the sweet treat I had in mind, but it'll do . . . for now." He winked. "Might I have some lemonade, Miss Libby?"

"Oh, pleathe, Mith Libby," one of the girls lisped. "Can we give him thome?"

"Of course." I tried my best not to stare at his chest, but it wasn't easy. He was making no such effort with regards to mine. "Would you get, um, Mr. Cameron a mug" — I glanced at the nametag of the girl next to me — "Amanda?" She trotted eagerly over to the cabinet. "Thanks, sweetie."

My hands shook slightly as I lifted the heavy pitcher to fill his pewter tankard. Amanda grabbed my hand and pulled me over to the door.

"Thith ith for you," she said.

I handed Cam the mug. He took a long gulp.

"*Mmmm.*" He licked his lips somewhat lasciviously. "Delicious."

"We made gingerbread too, if you want to wait and have some." Emily, a spectacled redhead, pushed her way to the front. "Or you can come back later. It'll be finished soon. How many quarter turns are left, Miss Libby?"

"Ah, would that I could, but I have to get back to my ship." Cam pointed into the distance, toward the water. "The *Anne-Marie*," he said reverently, placing a hand on his heart. "The most beautiful girl in the world. Well, second-most beautiful girl in the world, maybe," he amended.

"After Mith Libby?" Amanda asked.

"Smart girl." Cam winked. "I do want to try that gingerbread, though . . . I bet with so many talented cooks, it's delicious." He chewed his bottom lip thoughtfully, as the girls basked in his praise. Cam was a lady-killer with eight-year-old girls. I had a feeling there would be a lot of "I ♥ Cameron" doodled in notebooks tonight. I had to admit, it was really cute how nice he was to the girls. And how much they liked him. Unbelievably handsome, romantic, interested in history (obviously, as he was working at a museum), able to quote Shakespeare at the drop of a hat, *and* good with kids? Maybe dreams did come true. "Maybe . . . maybe Miss Libby could bring me a piece after camp?" he asked slyly.

"Maybe Miss Libby could!" one of the girls answered for me.

"Well, then." We locked eyes. "I'll see Miss Libby on the *Anne-Marie*." He handed back the mug, and his fingers brushed mine, shocking me like an electric current. Cam picked up the shirt he'd left on the woodpile and sauntered out of the garden, whistling a tune called "Cape Cod Girls" that I only recognized because Ashling had forced us to listen to her *Sailors' Songs and Sea Shanties* CD for "educational purposes" the other night.

"Miss Libby, I think you have a date!" Robin, who had first spotted him, squealed once he was out of sight.

"He's cuter than the Jonas Brothers," said another one, sighing.

"Cuter than the cowboy in the *Hannah Montana* movie," another one said, topping her.

"How about we check out how cute our gingerbread turned out?" I tried to turn the conversation away from the subject that was making me blush redder than the beets with which I'd recently become so well acquainted.

As the girls stood back, I carefully lifted the lid off with a set of tongs and, using my apron as a pot holder, extracted the tin of gingerbread.

"Now, how cute is that?" I marveled as I placed it on the kitchen table.

"Thuper-cute," Amanda agreed. It was perfect. I carefully cut steaming hot pieces that crumbled deliciously as we devoured them.

"This is really good," Emily said seriously. "The nutmeg really shines. I think it has a more pronounced flavor when you grate it by hand."

I stared. "How old are you?"

"Eight." She smiled, revealing two missing front teeth. "My dad writes for *Bon Appétit*."

Wow. Now that I had the world's teeniest, tiniest food critic on my hands, I'd really have to step up my game.

We finished the pan of gingerbread, minus one piece, which the girls demanded we save for Cam. I wrapped it in a clean kitchen towel and placed it in the warming oven on the side of the hearth. As the girls scrubbed out the Dutch oven under the water pump in the yard, I banked the fire and swept the ashes in the hearth. We spent the rest of the afternoon eating lunch outside on the green (another modern allowance: bagged lunch from home) and then at craft time in the parlor sketching out embroidery patterns. By the end of the day, all of the girls had outlines of boats drawn in their embroidery hoops, ready for needlework tomorrow. Just before two, I shuttled them back to the Welcome Center and handed them off to their respective moms, dads, and babysitters.

Two . . . two! The staff meeting/press conference/whatever it was! I ran back to the homestead as fast as my stays would let me, which was, admittedly, not very fast, and quickly changed into my Camden Harbor shirtdress and superfluous shorts. Now uncorseted, I sprinted back to the road, making much better time. As I rounded the corner to the administrative offices, an old woman yelled, "Put on some pants! Hussy!" She shook her fist. I think I'd just caught a glimpse of Ashling's future. Escaping into the offices before the old ladies could form a mob bearing pitchforks and torches, I made my way down the hall and skidded into the Oak Room. I slid into one of the few empty chairs in the back, next to a seat with a messenger bag slung over it. Ashling turned around from the front to glare at me, even though I wasn't technically late, as the meeting/whatever hadn't even started yet.

"Hello, Kitty."

Oh my God! It was the evil laugher in the Clark Kent glasses! He looked way too amused for his own good as he leaned over the seat next to me. I blushed and pointedly looked away. I had nothing to say to the buttface who'd left me stranded in a barrel. What a jerk.

"Me-yeow," he growled. "Angry kitty."

"This seat is taken," I said acidly, looking at the messenger bag.

"I know." He slid into the seat. "It's mine."

"Grrreeeaat," I said under my breath.

"I'm Garrett."

I opted to go with the silent treatment.

"And you are?"

I folded my hands demurely and pursed my lips.

"You realize I will keep calling you 'Kitty' if you don't tell me your name."

"Libby, okay?" I spat out. "Libby."

"Now, that wasn't so hard, was it?" He smirked. Ugh, he was just beyond smug.

"Nice T-shirt, by the way," I said sarcastically. "Another real winner." This one had a little insignia that read "Stargate SG-1" right where a normal person would have an alligator or a polo pony or something. And he had a button-down short-sleeved checked shirt on top of it, open, which was a look I'd only seen on TBS reruns of *Dawson's Creek*.

"Uh . . . thanks," he replied tentatively, like he wasn't sure if I was making fun of him or not. He pulled a little voice recorder out of his bag and set it on the table. Huh.

"What's that for?" I asked, curious. Garrett just kept getting weirder and weirder. "Are you taking notes for class? And why are you even here? Don't tell me you work at the museum."

"I'm a reporter," he announced proudly.

"For what, the school paper?"

"No." Garrett reddened. "It's not a school paper—it's a real paper, even if it is local. And I just graduated, anyway. And I'm—"

"Hey, guys, we're gonna go ahead and get started, okay?" A forty-something, slightly pudgy man at the front of the room called for attention. The room was packed with museum staff, but Maddie was the only one I recognized. "For those of you who don't know me, I'm Roger, the publicist here at Camden Harbor." Aha! Roger! This was the guy I'd heard fighting with Maddie about the ghost on my first day. "And at the request of the *Camden Crier*, I've called this press conference. Ed, you want to take it away?"

Before whoever this "Ed" was could say anything, Garrett spoke up. "Actually"—every head in the room swiveled toward

Garrett — "I called this press conference. My name is Garrett, and I'm interning at the *Camden Crier* this summer. I'm also" —he cleared his throat—"uh, Ed's son."

"What is it you want, boy?" an ancient man at the head of the table asked. Suze lobbed a piece of notebook paper at my nose. I uncrumpled it and read: "President Harrow, head of the museum." Wow, Suze was quick. She was going to make a very helpful librarian someday.

"Camden Harbor has a long history of suspicious, potentially paranormal activity." Garrett stood up. "With four similar sightings in just one month, however, whatever's going on with this 'ghostly sailor' on the *Lettie Mae* has the makings of a real story. I'd like your permission to do a piece on it"—he took a deep breath—"and to spend the summer sleeping on the boat to research it," he finished in a rush.

Madness broke out.

"This is a serious museum!" An old man with a bushy mustache banged his fist on the table. "Not a freak show! If we tell ghost stories and pander to thrill seekers, we compromise our integrity as an institution of research and education!"

"With all due respect, sir," Roger said as he cut through the crowd, "a story with a little popular appeal like this could really help boost our numbers. Let's be honest." The crowd settled down. "Camden Harbor is in serious trouble. We've been steadily losing money since the seventies, and with the country's current economic crisis, things are worse than ever before." A gloomy silence descended upon the room. "If we tell a little ghost story to bring a few people in, is that really so bad?" He shrugged. "All our research and integrity isn't worth a hill of beans if the museum goes under. All that really matters is getting people in the door. Once they're in, they'll learn something. If it's a ghost that brings 'em in, fine by me. When they're in, they're in." Roger sat back down—his words had clearly resonated.

"While I appreciate your concerns, Cecil," President Harrow said, acknowledging the man with the bushy mustache, "Roger makes a valid point." I decided that President Harrow may very well have been the oldest man in the world. "Let's give the boy a shot," he decided. "He's got gumption. And I've known your father a long time"—he nodded to the man toward the front, who must have been Ed—"and he's been the best editor in chief the *Crier* has had since Mitzi Taintor got out of the game in forty-seven."

From the sounds of the murmurings, most of the room agreed with the president.

"Someone should stay with him on the boat." A mousy-looking woman in a floral skirt at the front of the room spoke up for the first time.

Another piece of paper flew at my head: "Head librarian." Suze nodded toward the mousy woman. Aha.

"While I'm sure he is a very nice boy"—the head librarian smiled at Garrett—"I'm not comfortable with someone not on the museum staff staying on one of our boats, which is technically an artifact in our collections. One of the most expensive pieces we have, actually."

"Good point, Joanne." President Harrow nodded solemnly. "I agree. The boy needs someone on the boat."

Silence. The Camden Harbor staff shuffled their feet and

looked at their nails, clearly unwilling to give up their warm beds for a summer spent shipboard.

"Let's put one of the interns on it," Maddie suggested. Ah, yes. In the grand tradition of every company ever in the history of mankind, the job no one wanted fell to the interns.

"The boy is the obvious choice." President Harrow pointed a gnarled finger toward Neil, lurking in the back.

"He's not technically an intern," Maddie explained. "He has a federal grant; we only supply part of his funding, so we can't tell him where to live."

"Plus I need a flexible schedule to visit lighthouses," Neil added.

"What?" President Harrow asked.

"I NEED A FLEXIBLE SCHEDULE TO VISIT LIGHT-HOUSES," Neil shouted.

The president covered his ears. "Oh, I heard you. I just wanted to make sure everybody else did."

The marine biologists next to Neil, two sun-browned, windblown, healthy-looking girls in anoraks whom I'd never seen before, even though I supposedly lived with them, begged off on similar grounds.

"Then that leaves my girls." Maddie smiled encouragingly at the three of us.

"Live . . . boy . . . boat . . . bunk," Suze babbled incoherently, blanching.

I was getting an idea. This could be my ticket out of Hell House! Sure, Garrett was beyond annoying, but I was pretty sure he wouldn't put shampoo in my bed. Or steal my strawberry-banana yogurt. Or collect hair from my brush for a voodoo doll, which I currently suspected Ashling of doing.

"Will there be modern conveniences aboard ship?" Ashling asked stridently.

"Like what?" Garrett furrowed his brow. "A shower?"

"No showers for you!" President Harrow cackled.

"Whoever lives on the ship can use the bathrooms at the intern house," Maddie added quickly. "And the kitchen. Whenever they want."

"Electronics?" Ashling prompted.

"Well, uh, I'll have my laptop, voice recorder, cell phone, digital camera, video camera, and—"

"Susannah Fennyweather cannot exist near digital recording devices. It would compromise the historical integrity of both my interpretation and her existence as a separate, sentient being. Yes, you should probably go with a *less* dedicated historical interpreter." Here she looked pointedly toward me.

"Ashling, it's not that I'm not dedicated—" I started.

"Then you explain that Hello Kitty underwear," Garrett said under his breath, smirking.

"Plus," Ashling interrupted, "I don't think my boyfriend, Martin Cheeseman, would approve of my living with another man, so you should probably ask someone single." Another pointed look toward me.

"*You* have a *boyfriend?*" That was me.

"Martin *Cheeseman?*" That was Garrett.

Ashling smiled smugly as if she'd just confirmed that yes, indeed, her boyfriend was, in fact, Brad Pitt.

"How do you even know I'm single?" I asked suspiciously.

"Please," Ashling scoffed, "you were practically *licking* those Squaddies." She pronounced "Squaddies" with the sort of disgust usually reserved for "poop" or "pedophiles."

"I didn't lick anyone!" I squawked. "I repeat, I did not lick *anyone.*" I leaned into Garrett's tape recorder. "Let the record show that Libby Kelting did not lick anyone."

"This, uh, isn't a courtroom." He scooted the recorder away from me.

"Then why do I feel like I'm being judged?" I glared in Ashling's general direction.

"Also, as a whaler's daughter"—Ashling cleared her throat—"Susannah Fennyweather would be all too aware that many mariners believed that a woman aboard ship brought bad luck."

"I'll do it!" I cried, before this could go any further. "Sign me up!"

"Oh, super," Garrett muttered.

"Hey! I said I'd do it. I'm doing you a favor! What is your problem?" I demanded. I mean, he shouldn't have had any objections. I was the one sacrificing myself! I'd probably go blind after a summer spent with someone so sartorially challenged. But as hard as it was to believe, he wasn't as bad as Ashling. Garrett was a pain in the butt, but not downright malicious.

"I don't want some little Nancy Drew–wannabe tagging along." He shrugged. "I don't need a babysitter. I can do this by myself."

Nancy Drew. Nancy Drew?!

"Ohhh, um, ooookay, Clark Kent. Why don't you just head on back to the *Daily Planet* where you belong and foil a caper there, okay?"

"*Pfff!*" he spat. "If I'm foiling anything, the last thing I need is Cat Grant dragging me down."

"Who?" I asked, confused.

"She's the gossip columnist at the *Daily Planet,* blond, pushy. She was introduced as a potential love interest for Clark Kent in *Adventures of Superman* number 424, and . . . Never mind," Garrett trailed off, embarrassed.

"Nerd," I muttered just loud enough for Garrett to hear me. I mean, really. Who memorizes the issue numbers of comic books? Someone with no life, that's who.

"I like this Nancy Drew–Hardy Boys angle," the guy I was pretty sure was Ed said, jumping in. "Boy reporter and his girl Friday fighting crime in quaint New England town! Good spin."

"Girl Friday?" I objected. "Um, if anything, he's totally my . . . boy Friday."

"I don't want to spend my summer in a Nancy Drew–Hardy Boys Crossover Mystery Super Spectacular," Garrett shouted. "I want this to be a piece of serious journalism."

"What, I can't do serious?" I asked. "I can totally do serious."

"You have got to be joking," Ashling said, snickering.

"Like I said, I really don't want some little high school kid tagging along," Garrett spoke over Ashling.

"Excuse me?!" I spluttered. "Like you're *so* much more mature than me because you're a year older. You've been out of high school for what, a week?"

"Not the point," he muttered.

"Listen," Maddie interrupted, "Garrett can't stay on the boat alone. Libby's willing to stay on the boat. Problem solved. End of discussion."

"But—" Garrett interjected.

"I agree," Ed said. "End of discussion."

"Then it's settled," President Harrow concluded. "They can bunk in the fo'c's'le."

"The what-sil?" I asked, slightly panicky. "The what and a hey now?"

"Hee-hee!" President Harrow tittered. "Dirty mind, young lady!"

Someone hissed, "Slut." I took a wild guess—Ashling.

"The fo'c's'le," Garrett explained exasperatedly. "*Fo'c's'le* stands for 'forecastle.' It's the part at the front of the ship, and there are two bunks under there on the *Lettie Mae*."

"And it's the only part of the ship closed to the public," Maddie added. "It's perfect. There's trunk space under the bunk to store your gear."

"That might be a problem for Libby," Ashling said. "Can she bring a shoe rack?"

"Not a problem," I said, overriding her objection. "Not a problem at all."

"Then there are no problems." President Harrow looked around for something, eventually selecting a leather-bound volume from the bookshelf behind him. "You can move onto the *Lettie Mae* this weekend." He smacked the book on the table, a makeshift gavel, and yelled joyfully, "Meeting adjourned!"

Everyone gathered their things and started shuffling out.

"Um, Garrett?" I tugged on his sleeve. "Can we talk? Outside?"

"Sure." He nodded testily, before we were swept away on a sea of museum staffers.

"Hey, um, Garrett?" I waved. "Uh, Garrett? Over here."

"I'm, ugh, coming." He pushed his way through the crowd and met me under the pine tree I'd staked out.

"Listen, Garrett—"

"Why do you keep saying my name like it's in air quotes?" he interrupted.

"What are you talking about?" I snapped.

"You keep saying 'Garrett' like it's *allegedly* my name."

"Maybe because it's not a name, but a small Parisian attic where writers live?"

"Oh, as opposed to a brand of canned pumpkin owned by the Nestlé corporation?" he shot back.

We glared at each other. "Listen, 'Garrett,'" I began again, and this time I actually used air quotes. He grimaced behind his stupid Clark Kent glasses but didn't say anything. "I know you don't want me there, but I'm sorry. You don't have a choice. I'm going to be there. So we're just going to have to make this work."

"Why?" He gestured wildly and then readjusted his grip on his messenger bag as it flapped. "Why are you doing this? Why do you need to be there? Can't they find someone else to babysit me if they have to? Or can't you just *say* you're there and leave me alone?"

"Not an option, 'Garrett.'" Ha-ha! Each time I air-quoted, he seemed progressively more annoyed. "I do need to be there because I am living with a cat-loving, shoe-hating historical interpreter who wants me dead. And as impossible as it is to believe, *you* are the lesser of two evils."

"I'm flattered," he muttered.

"So deal with it. It's happening." I spun on my heel and

stalked off. "See you shipboard, roomie!" I called over my shoulder.

"Can't wait," he said sarcastically.

I stopped. "Hey, Garrett, 1998 called—it wants its outfit back."

He did a double take, then said, "Incidentally, when 1998 was on the phone, it also asked for that joke back."

My jaw dropped. I snapped it shut and went off to finish my sentence in the Hell House without another word. I had the sinking suspicion that I'd just leaped out of the frying pan and into the fire.

chapter four

Needle (noun): 1. A small, slender, usually steel instrument that has an eye for thread at one end and that is used for sewing. 2. A teasing or gibing remark.

One definition described my days at Camden Harbor, the other, my evenings that last week living with Ashling. I was thrilled when Friday afternoon rolled around. As soon as camp ended, I'd be moving my things out of the house and into the harbor. The late-afternoon sun slanted through the parlor windows as we worked on our samplers, and I was filled with peace.

"Miss Libby, Miss Libby!" one of the girls shrieked. *Boom* —peace shattered. "*That boy* is back!"

The rest of the girls screamed, chucked their samplers willy-nilly over the settee, and ran to the window.

"Thith time he'th brought *flowerth*," Amanda lisped, amid a chorus of *ooh*s.

I stooped to pick up a few samplers, straightened, and looked out the window. Cam was coming up the front walk, with a bouquet of flowers in one hand and a small white bag in the other. Not only did he actually have his navy jacket on, buttoned, but he'd also added a waistcoat and even a casually tied cravat—every inch the proper gentleman.

"Miss Libby, I believe he's come courting," Emily said, squinting through her glasses.

"A thuuuiter." More *oohs*. A what? Oh, "a suitor."

Cam rapped a little pattern on the door: *knock, knock, knock, knock, knock — knock knock.*

The girls screamed and dove for the settee, picking up whatever sampler was nearest. They were almost interchangeable, anyway — I'd sketched out patterns of all the different ships in the harbor for them to embroider with indigo-dyed linen thread, and they'd all picked the *Anne-Marie*. Surprise, surprise.

"Get the door, Miss Libby!" they said collectively with giggles, pretending — and failing — to be very involved in their needlework. "Get it, get it, get it!"

I paused to check myself out in the hall mirror. I hadn't seen Cam since he'd chopped our wood. How lucky that I'd just happened to choose the pretty pink flowered dress today! Taking a deep breath, I flung open the heavy wooden door.

I was almost finished with *Northanger Abbey*, mostly because I'd discovered Ashling talked to me less if I was reading, so for lack of a better option, I'd started scouting out the romance novels in the house "library" for my next book. I swear to God, the cover art for *Let Sleeping Rogues Lie* had leaped off the page and shown up on my doorstep.

"Miss Libby," he said bowing deeply. "I've come calling." He grinned, shaking the hair out of his eyes, and I was hit with the full force of how unbearably, impossibly gorgeous he was. Yes, sure, the (very small) handful of boys who'd been interested in me in the past weren't total trolls, but they had left me completely unprepared for the movie-star-hot manifestation of my dream man. It was like I'd opened a door to the magical fantasyland in my head. I was frozen to the step like the little delft milkmaid on the shelf in the parlor.

"Let him in!" one of the girls shrieked. The rest took it up, chanting, "Let him in! Let him in!"

"I think you'd better let me in. Or it might get ugly in there," he said, widening his eyes.

"I think I'd better," I agreed, and, heart hammering, I let him in. I closed the door behind me and led him to the parlor.

"Ladies." Cam swept an elaborate bow. The girls giggled. "Miss Libby," he stage-whispered loud enough for them to overhear, "can they have candy?" He shook the little white bag.

"Please! Please, Miss Libby, please can we have candy? Please, please, please!" they all begged.

"Of course." The day was almost over. If they got hyper, their parents would have to deal with it. And how cute was it that he'd brought them candy! Cam went over to the girls and gave them each one of those swirly-stick candies they sold in the gift shop.

"Mithter Cameron?" Amanda asked as she pulled out a strawberry swirl-stick candy. "Where were you all week? Why did you thay away?"

"Ah, fair lady, I was nursing a wound." The girls gasped. "A broken heart." More, louder dismayed gasps.

"Who broke your heart? Tell me. Who. Who did it?" Natalie, one of the older, pushier girls, demanded.

"Why, as much as it pains me to say it, our very own Miss Libby." He shook his head sadly. "She never stopped by with my gingerbread."

Ohh, right—with all the ghost excitement, the sparring with Garrett, and the possibility of escaping Ashling, I'd completely forgotten. Cam's gingerbread must have still been wrapped in the towel in the warming oven.

"Oh, Mith Libby, how could you?" Amanda whispered painfully amid general noises denouncing my villainy.

"Yes, Miss Libby, how could you?" Cam echoed, mock-wounded. "Hasn't she been naughty?"

Wow, I hoped the kids missed the subtext.

"She should be punished," Natalie said grumpily.

"I was thinking the same thing." Cam looked like he was about to burst, trying not to laugh. "But even though she doesn't deserve it," Cam said, composing himself, "I've decided to forgive her. And be nice. Because that's just the kind of guy I am. Miss Libby"—he displayed the flowers with a flourish—"these are for you."

The girls paused in unwrapping their candies to sigh, collectively, "Awwww."

"They're beautiful, Cam." I accepted them, blushing. They really were. A boy had never brought me flowers before. Dev was wrong—chivalry wasn't dead. Gentlemen *did* exist. And I was face-to-face with living proof. "Thank you."

"You should probably put those in water." Emily shook her candy stick at me.

"How right you are," Cam said, steering me toward the kitchen. "Let me help you, Miss Libby."

"But the girls, I—"

"Oh, they'll be fine for a minute," he insisted, quashing my protest. "They have candy."

Cam took a jug from the kitchen, filled it with water from the pump out back, and placed it on the kitchen table. The minute I'd put the flowers in the jug, Cam pulled me away from the table, brought my head toward his, and kissed me. Deeply.

"Cam." I broke away breathlessly, completely taken aback by how sudden this was. "The girls. They're in the other room. We can't. Not here, I—"

"What are you doing after this?" he asked, cradling my face in his hands.

"I'm—I'm moving into a bunk on the *Lettie Mae*," I explained, trying to conjure a coherent thought out of thin air even though my brain appeared to have shut down. "I have to get my things out of the house and into the boat."

"The *Lettie Mae*?" He wrinkled his nose distastefully. "I think you're moving into a bunk on the wrong ship." Cam stroked my cheek. "You'd have a lot more fun on the *Anne-Marie*. I promise."

"Oohhhh, Miss Liiiiiiiiiiiibbby," one of the girls said in a loud singsong from the other room, "what are you dooooooo-iiiiiiiiiing?" Giggle explosion.

"I—I have to go back in." I gestured to the parlor, trying to break away, even though it was the last thing I wanted to do.

"I'll help you move." He kissed me again, quickly, fiercely. "Change and meet me at the wharf at two forty-five."

"Two forty-five," I whispered back, as he vaulted out the kitchen window. The man knew how to make an exit.

I tried to collect myself, but my heart was pounding so loudly, I was afraid the girls would hear it. Or that it might burst forth from my stays and leap straight out of my chest. But somehow I managed to keep all my vital organs in the right places as I collected the samplers, put them in the cabinet, and took the girls back to the Welcome Center in a maelstrom of Cam-related teasing and giggling.

There wasn't any camp on the weekends, so the goodbyes

took a little longer. Eventually, everyone had been hugged and handed off, so I was free to hustle my bustle (literally) back to the Bromleigh Homestead. As I changed into my standard-issue polo and nonexistent khakis, I cursed the fates for condemning me to this hideous shirtdress and myself for not having the foresight to smuggle in some makeup. This was a sort of/almost/kind of *date,* for Pete's sake, with the hottest guy I ever had or probably ever would cross paths with, and I was going dressed as a half-nudist man. With no eyelashes.

Taking a page out of Scarlett O'Hara's book, I pinched my cheeks and bit my lips, and then added my own personal touch: the sooty swipe of ashy eye shadow. It would have to do. I locked up the house and made my way toward the wharf, which was at the corner of the museum closest to my house. It served as the unofficial barrier between the historical harbor at the museum and the working harbor in town.

I couldn't believe Cam had offered to help me move — how could someone so hot also be so sweet? Not like that idiot Garrett, who would barely even fish me out of a barrel, let alone move my hair-care products to a schooner. Not that Garrett had anything to do with this — who knew why he had randomly popped into my head.

Cam was leaning against an old wooden pole in the water, squinting into the late-afternoon sun, and pushing all thoughts of Garrett from my mind. Somehow Cam even managed to look good in the stupid Camden Harbor uniform, which defied all the natural laws of physics.

"Already got her pants off?" He smirked, looping his thumbs casually through his khaki belt loops as he pushed off the pole and ambled over to me. "My kind of girl."

"No, no, I'm wearing shorts." Blushing like crazy, I lifted my shirt to show him. "See? Perfectly respectable chinos. They're conservative. They're J.Crew."

Cam laughed. "God, you have no idea how cute you are, do you?" He slung his arm around my shoulder, and we walked together off the museum grounds. "Which way's your house, babe?"

Babe? Babe? Oh my God, I was "babe"! I was also hyper-ventilating slightly. Being this close to him, especially with the memory of that kitchen kiss searing my brain, was almost too much to take. He smelled sort of salty, like a sea breeze, which should have been gross but was inexplicably intoxicating.

We chatted—well, mostly he chatted, and I nodded—as I showed him down the sidewalk to my house. The five-minute walk felt a lot shorter without Ashling, much to my chagrin. All too soon, Cam dropped his arm as I pushed open the front door.

"Careful!" I warned. "Don't let it slam; it—"

Too late. It slammed shut and wobbled dangerously but held.

"Libby!" Ashling called shrilly. "HOW many times I have told you NOT to slam the door! And I know it's you!"

Cam raised his eyebrows.

"Welcome to my nightmare." I gestured grandly. "Come on, you can hang out in the living room while I get my stuff together. It'll only take a minute."

I'd decided to use my third of my room in the house as my closet, and only to take the bare essentials—Camden Harbor uniform, underwear, toiletries, Chucks, PJs, bathing suit, flip-flops, a book—on the boat with me. I figured that way, everybody won: Ashling and Suze got more space, and I could turn my bed into a shoe rack.

"You might need to hold my hand," Cam whispered. "It's scary in here."

I took his hand and pulled him down the skinny hallway to the living room.

Neil's long limbs were draped all over the couch, extending off both sides. He shifted slightly over his radishes and hummus to reveal a heavily bandaged shoulder.

"Neil!" I gasped. "What happened?"

"I got shot," he said through a mouthful of radish, muting the old *Monty Python* sketches he'd been watching.

"What? Shot?" In my seventeen years, I've run across very few situations for which the word *flabbergasted* was appropriate. This, however, was one of them.

"Turns out some of the last living lighthouse keepers are very, um, territorial about the lighthouses they keep."

"Yikes."

"A lighthouse keeper shot you?" Cam looked impressed. "That's awesome."

"Are you okay?" I asked. "I can't believe you were shot!"

"Shot with what I believe was an 1873 Winchester still mostly in working order—what a find!" Neil finished excitedly.

"I'm, um, happy for you?" I wasn't totally sure what the correct response was when someone had enjoyed a near-death experience involving a rare historical artifact.

"Yeah, I was really lucky," he continued. "If the gun had been in mint condition, I would probably be dead. Thank God for pH deterioration, right?" He chuckled.

"Uh, right," I agreed.

Ashling appeared in the kitchen door frame like a malevolent ghost in a floral apron, stirring a large chipped mixing bowl.

"Libby, I'm not sure I'm comfortable with boys in the house," she drawled.

"Um, hello, there's always a boy in the house. One lives here. What about Neil?" I pointed to him.

"A necessary evil." Neil frowned into his radishes. "I don't want you parading your men through here at all hours of the night."

"It's three in the afternoon! And one guy is not a parade." I turned to Cam, blushing. "There's no parade."

"I'm Cam." He stuck out his hand to Ashling.

"Do you work at the museum?" she asked suspiciously, slooowly extending her arm.

"Yep. Demo squad." He jokingly saluted.

Ashling withdrew her hand so fast a casual observer might have thought he'd said "sewage treatment plant." She hissed and turned away, like Dracula facing a mirror. Or a cat in a bath.

"Cam, I'll be right back with my stuff." I sighed. He was going to run screaming for the hills.

"Wait." Ashling stopped me, disappeared into the kitchen for a moment, and then returned with an envelope. It had my name written in ballpoint pen on the front. "These came for us today. It should have everything you need. So you won't ever need to come back." She returned to the kitchen.

I jammed the envelope in my back pocket as I grabbed the rest of my things out of the bathroom and stuffed them on top of the pink duffle bag I'd packed the night before. I was steps away from freedom.

"Ready to go?" I asked, coming back to the living room. Cam was leaning against the wall, arms folded, watching *Monty Python.*

"That it?" He jerked his thumb in the direction of my bag.

"Yep."

"A girl who packs light." He picked it up off my shoulder and swung it easily over his. He was even carrying my bag! So gallant. "You see something new every day." Cam readjusted the bag. "Let's do this."

"Bye, Neil." I waved. "Get better soon!" He waved back with a radish, and Cam and I headed down the hall. Suze popped out of the bedroom, squeaked, and popped right back in. We left.

"Wow"—Cam shook his head—"what a bunch of freak shows."

"They're . . . different," I said diplomatically. "But aside from Ashling, they're not that bad."

"Not that bad?" He snorted. "Andre the Giant, the hostile bitch, and the mute virgin? Please. You are way too nice. Thank God you're getting out of there, Libs. You're gonna love living on a ship. There's nothing like it."

He waxed rhapsodic about boats and maritime life the rest of the walk over. Yes, my former roommates were weird, but I thought Cam was being a little harsh. Zoning out somewhere around the time we got to discussing the mizzen, I remembered the envelope I'd stuck in my pocket. I quickly opened it and unfolded the typed sheet of paper within.

It was a "Camden Harbor Summer of Fun Social Calendar."

I quickly skimmed it: Sea Shanty Showdown, Fourth of July Lobsterfest (Featuring Fireworks!), and, finally, the End-of-Season Costume Ball (Period Costume Mandatory).

"Oh yeah." Cam was reading over my shoulder. "The Showdown's coming up. It's awesome. Starts in the boathouse, then moves out to the dock. There's beer and stuff. Wanna come with?"

"I'd love to, um, come with."

He laughed at me. It didn't really sound like my kind of thing, as it involved "beer and stuff," but it was historical, right? I'd be fine. Plus, it was a date! With Cam! At least, I thought so . . . I mean, sure, he didn't technically *say* it, but if we were going together, that meant we were *going together,* right?

We'd arrived. "Where we going?" Cam ran a hand through his hair.

"The fo'c's'le," I pronounced carefully. I'd Googled it earlier. "*Mmm,* cozy."

He wasn't kidding. We made our way up the gangplank of the *Lettie Mae* and down the smallest set of stairs I'd ever seen, passing through a narrow hall into a space that was more cupboard than room. Garrett was already lying in the bunk on the left-hand side. He sat up so fast, he hit his head on the ceiling with a sickening crack.

"OW!" Garrett rubbed his head. "Jesus Christ, I think I saw stars. Like in a cartoon," he muttered absent-mindedly.

"You didn't tell me you were living *with* someone, babe." Cam dropped my duffle roughly to the floor. Garrett grimaced as the word "babe" left Cam's lips.

"No, no it's not like that!" I rushed to explain.

"Definitely not like that," Garrett said so firmly, I was almost a little insulted. He climbed down the little wooden ladder that led to his bunk to stand in the two square feet of floor space between the bunks. He folded his arms across the "I am the Fifth Cylon" printed on his chest, whatever that meant, and leaned against the ladder.

"Garrett is, um, investigating," I explained.

"Investigating?" Garrett repeated. "Like I said, Nancy Drew, this is not *The Secret of the Old Clock*—"

"Sorry, sorry, whatever!" I interrupted. God, he took himself *so seriously.* And he wrote for a newspaper that probably like all of fifteen people read! "Garrett, our intrepid *Camden Crier* reporter, is writing a piece of journalism so serious, it is second only to a treatise on Fallujah, except the subject happens to be a *ghost* instead of war crimes."

"A ghost?" Cam chuckled. "That's cute, Nancy." This was addressed to Garrett, not me. "I see you've got your flashlight in case the big, scary ghost comes to get you."

"And the museum decided," I continued, before Garrett could say anything, "that he couldn't stay on the boat alone. Not being museum staff and all. And it kind of fell to me, because nobody wanted to do it."

"Shocker." Cam snorted. "Well, at least since it's Garrett, I know I don't have to worry about anything happening between the two of you." Garrett stiffened but said nothing. "Later, Libs." Cam slung an arm around my shoulder and deposited a smacking kiss on my cheek, eyes on Garrett the whole time. "And you'll definitely get a good night's rest. This one'll put you right to sleep. Ask him to tell you about *Battlestar Galac-*

tica." He left the fo'c's'le, laughing all the way up the stairs and out of the ship.

"*Battlestar Galactica,*" Garrett muttered distractedly as he climbed back into his bunk to give me room to unpack. "*Battlestar Galactica!*" That was more of a declaration of outrage. He started fiddling with a flashlight, screwing and unscrewing the part where the batteries went in. "You know, *Time* magazine named it one of the One Hundred Best Television Shows of All Time. It's been in the *New York Times*' Top Ten list every year since it debuted. And it's been nominated for several writing, acting, and directing Emmys, in addition to the ones it *won* for visual effects. I don't understand why this country has such a weird prejudice against science fiction. Because it involves interplanetary travel, it's automatically crap?"

I realized he was waiting for an answer. "Um . . ." I finished stuffing the rest of my things in the whitewashed trunk bench. "I like watching things where people attend English country dances and fall in love, so I'm, um, probably not your target audience."

"Anyone involved with Cam is definitely not my target audience," he said so quietly, I wasn't sure if I was supposed to hear it.

"Listen," I said, "I'm all unpacked, so I'm gonna hang out on deck. If you want to stay in this cave, that is totally fine with me, but I'm going up. You do whatever you want."

I grabbed my book and headed up, leaving him in the bunk, hoping he didn't follow. Up the steps and on deck, out of the claustrophobic cabin, I decided I liked boats. The *Lettie Mae* was a small ship, for a schooner, and the weather-beaten wooden planks fit snugly together. "My, she's yar," I said to no one in particular. It was the only nautical term I knew, because Katharine Hepburn had said it in *Philadelphia Story.*

I went straight up to the bow at the front of the ship, resisted the urge to have my very own *Titanic* "I'm the king of the world!" moment, and sank down in a little ball, snuggling against the side of the ship. The bow was very cozy. Hours flew by as I sat there reading, totally immersed in the world of the book.

"That looks sort of thick for *People* magazine," an unwelcome voice said snarkily, interrupting my reading. Jesus. Why did everyone at this museum think I was stupid? Did they not have well-dressed blondes in Maine? This was getting ridiculous. But when I looked up, mentally prepping a biting comeback, I came face-to-face with a horrifying sight.

"Oh my God," I said, gasping, "you did not seriously bring those Hobbit feet up here."

"What?" Garrett was standing above me, little digital video camera in hand, displaying the biggest, hairiest, most terrifying feet I had ever seen. "Wait, you know what a Hobbit is?"

"Yes, I know what a Hobbit is. I'm not pop-culturally challenged. I saw *Lord of the Rings.* I was even in the Orlando Bloom fan club in fourth grade. I had his poster in my locker. Oh my *God,* can you *please* put on some socks?!"

"Orlando Bloom portrayed Legolas, the Sindar Elf of the Woodland Realm. Not a Hobbit," Garrett said seriously. "And in my opinion, his performance was one of the weaker ones in the fellowship—"

"Oh my God, I don't care, whatever! Socks, shoes, something, please! I am instituting a new policy! Shoes or socks must be worn in communal areas!"

"Fine, fine!" Finally he stomped away and then returned a minute or two later, feet thankfully encased in Converses. Phew.

"Much better," I muttered.

"So what are you reading?" He crouched down to my level. Curses. Why did he insist on socializing? Well, it's not like I could dodge him forever. I had to spend the rest of the summer with him in very close quarters. So I supposed I just had to make the best of it. "Something about shoes and lipstick?" he said sarcastically.

Grrrrrr.

"*Northanger Abbey.*" I showed him the cover. A small woman in a black dress made her way down a long, maroon-carpeted hallway. "No shoes, no lipstick. Fun fact: Sometimes girls read things that aren't magazines or related to *Gossip Girl* in any way, shape, or form. There you go. A little bit of trivia, free from me to you."

"Is that . . . Jane Austen?" he asked. He sounded surprised, which only annoyed me more. Both that he knew Jane Austen had written it and that he didn't think I'd be reading it.

"Impressive," I said approvingly, albeit very grudgingly. "Most people haven't heard of it."

"I, uh, read it on the cover," he admitted, laughing.

"That's okay." I laughed with him, in spite of myself. "Like I said, most people, especially boys, haven't heard of it. Let me guess: you had to read *Pride and Prejudice* in, oh, let's say junior English in high school, and that pretty much sums up your Jane Austen experience?"

"Pretty much." He nodded. "Is this one good? I mean, they

didn't make it into a movie with Keira Knightley, so it can't be *that* good." After a moment or two, the ghost of a smile flitted across his face, and I realized he was joking. "It's sort of, um, unusual that you're reading it, right?"

"Sort of, yeah," I agreed. "The really unusual thing is that it's my favorite. I don't think I know anyone else whose favorite it is."

"Why is it your favorite?" He folded his knees into his chest. One had a Band-Aid on it, which looked sort of funny on his big knees, like he was the world's largest six-year-old boy. And it appeared to be a Transformers Band-Aid. Oh my God. So he *was* the world's largest six-year-old boy.

"Catherine, the heroine, has kind of an overactive imagination. She loves these dark, mysterious gothic novels and sees herself as the heroine of one. And you should be the heroine of your own life, you know? I like her. She's feisty. Funny. I think the best word is . . . irrepressible," I decided. "And the hero, Henry Tilney? I like how sarcastic he is. He's smart, well read . . . the two of them seem like people I'd want to be friends with. Like real people, who would actually fall in love. Who you could see having a life together. I mean, sure, yes, Sexypants Darcy, everyone loves him — I get it. I like him too. But he's just so . . . aloof. Could you really hang out with Mr. Darcy? Sometimes I don't really know if I could. Henry Tilney, though, you could totally just shoot the shit with."

"An interesting theory." Garrett nodded. "But you know," he said seriously, "I might be wrong, but I *think* Mr. Darcy's first name was Fitzwilliam, not *Sexypants*. I did only get a B on that test, though, so I don't know . . ."

I blushed and decided to steer the conversation away from sexy anything. "This is the real reason I fell in love with it, though. My favorite line:

> "History, real solemn history, I cannot be inter-
> ested in. . . . I read it a little as a duty, but it tells me
> nothing that does not either vex or weary me. The
> quarrels of popes and kings, with wars or pestilen-
> ces, in every page; the men all so good for nothing,
> and hardly any women at all—it is very tiresome."

"What?" He wrinkled his nose, confused. "You're working at a museum. Don't you like history?"

"Yes." I nodded. "Of course I like it. I love it. I know, it seems contradictory, but this is how I feel about a lot of history. I don't like 'solemn' history either—wars and plagues and dates. History isn't an endless parade of facts. There's so much more to it than that! Catherine would have loved the history that *I* love. History is just stories—I mean think about it, *story* is right in the word—history is the life stories of millions and millions of people. Real people, living, beautiful, ugly, wonderful, horrible, messy, complicated human lives. War isn't just the names of a victor and a loser and the date it happened, but *who* was that victor, not just on the battlefield, but in the barn or the bedroom, you know? *Why* was he the victor? You know how they say truth is stranger than fiction? All the greatest stories in the world are things that have *actually happened.* History isn't dull or dry or dead or boring—when you look at it like that, it's the most alive thing there is! You know?" He was staring. "God, I'm sorry." I blushed. "I got a little carried away. I usually do, when I talk about history." So carried away that I'd completely forgotten who I was talking to. And that he was a lame sci-fi freak with gross feet who thought I was stupid.

"No, no! That's great!" Garrett rushed in. "I think it's great that you're so passionate about it. I was just . . . just thinking how *weird* it was that you said that, because that's basically exactly how I feel about journalism. Except I've never been able to articulate it so well." He grinned wryly.

"That was hardly articulate," I countered.

"I mean," he went on, "when you think about it, history is just journalism plus a hundred years, give or take. Right?"

"Yeah, I guess it is." I smiled. "You're right. I'd never thought about it like that."

The sun had started to set over the bow of the ship, bathing us in color.

"Red sky at night, sailor's delight," I said softly.

Garrett's face darkened, like he'd just remembered something. "So . . . you and Cameron?"

"Oh, um, I don't know." I blushed. "I've only known him for like a week."

"So you're not dating?" he asked brusquely.

"I, um, I don't think so. I don't really know," I admitted. "He, um, asked me to, um, 'come with' to this Sea Shanty Showdown thing, but I don't really know what that means . . ."

"Cameron was being vague? What a surprise." He stood up abruptly. "Trust me. I've known Cameron for a long time. You'd be better off if it meant nothing. Much better off." Garrett brushed some nonexistent specks of dirt off his shorts.

"The sun's almost set. I'm gonna go downstairs and see if anything shows up."

"Wait." I got up to join him. "How does this work? Are you going to stake out all night long? Do I need to like supervise? Do I have to watch you the whole time? Or can you just promise me you're not going to pull a Guy Fawkes and blow this mother up?"

"No, you don't have to watch me. And Guy Fawkes failed, anyway."

I followed him down into the hold.

"Oh, I know. I assumed you would fail in your attempt, as all the gunpowder in here is fake. That was part of the metaphor." I mean, obviously.

He went into the fo'c's'le, and returned with two battery-powered portable camping lamps. "Here. This is for you. It'll get really dark really fast, and all of the oil lamps in here are fake—and any kind of flame would be a safety hazard, anyway." He handed it over.

"Are you going to stay up all night?" I asked.

"Oh, I don't know." He sighed. "The ghost has only ever been sighted in the early evening, around now, but that might just be because no one was on the ship later. So I guess I'll just hang out with my video camera until I get tired."

"Listen," I said halfheartedly, "if you want me to do a shift or something, I guess I could. You could wake me up, if you want."

"No. No, that's fine." He brushed past me and went deeper into the ship. "Good night."

"Um, good night," I called after his retreating back.

Inside the fo'c's'le, which was, except for the camping lantern, pitch-black, I changed into heart-patterned boxers and a Hello Kitty T-shirt. After placing the light and my book up on the bunk, I climbed up the ladder and got into bed.

It was sort of creepy in there. Okay, really creepy. The camping light cast all sorts of eerie shadows into the gloom as the boat rocked gently, and you could hear the wind whistling from outside. Not that I ever in a million years would have admitted to Garrett that I was a little freaked out, but I was. Really freaked out.

I tried to read but couldn't concentrate. What was Garrett's problem with Cam? He had gotten all weird and shifty, and we'd been having a perfectly pleasant conversation about Jane Austen and history and stuff. Cam was such a nice guy. I mean, hello, he carried my duffle and he wanted me to "come with" to the Sea Shanty Showdown! That definitely meant something. Plus, I'm sorry, Garrett, sci-fi *is* lame. Fact.

Several hours of sort of reading later, the door to the fo'c's'le slowly creaked open. I screamed so loudly that it was a wonder the camping lantern didn't shatter. An ominous disembodied voice rumbled through from the other side: "Hello, Kitty."

The door swung open the rest of the way to reveal Garrett.

"You are a jerk!" I yelled, chucking my pillow at him. "I almost had a freaking heart attack!"

"Sorry, sorry." He laughed. "I couldn't resist."

"Jerk!" I yelled again. "Now give me my goddamn pillow back so I can keep beating you!"

"I think, no." He set up his camping lantern next to his bed. "That is not in my best interest."

"Fine. You know what? Fine." I huffed. "Whatever. We're

done with this." I shut off my lamp and pulled the blanket over my head.

"Good night, Kitty."

Garrett softly lobbed the pillow onto my bed, turned out his lamp, and went to sleep.

chapter five

"Good morrow, good woman."

I looked up from the bed of pansies I'd been mucking around in. "Hey, Ashling." I gritted my teeth.

"I know not what means this 'Ashling'!" she shouted, nostrils flaring. "What creature or species or man or beast an 'Ashling' may be, know not I! I am Susannah Fennyweather, daughter of Horatio Fennyweather, a gentlewoman of Camden Towne!"

She pronounced the "e" in the old-fashioned spelling of town, making it sound like "townie." I had never before encountered Ashling in full Susannah Fennyweather mode, and it was a sight to behold. She was brass-buttoned up to her neck in a mud-brown gown, her hat had so many feathers it looked like it was about to take flight, and she brandished a parasol like a weapon.

"Mith Libby"—Amanda popped up from somewhere in the general vicinity of my knees—"whoth thith?" The other girls stopped picking flowers and came over to join me by the fence that separated the homestead garden from the lane. Now that the samplers were done, I'd decided to move on to pressed flowers, so today we were out picking. This decision obviously had nothing to do with the fact that Cam had stopped by again to chop wood. Well, at the moment, he was leaning against the house, eating a piece of the applesauce molasses spice cake we'd made that morning, but he had been chopping wood.

"Well, girls, this is Susannah Fennyweather, daughter of Horatio Fennyweather, gentlewoman of Camden *Town*." I made it a point to markedly *not* pronounce an "e." "Susannah, this is Amanda and Robin and—"

"I care not." She cut me off. "And you shall address me as Miss Fennyweather, not presume to condone the usage of my Christian name."

"Um, eeuw," said one of the girls, and a few others giggled.

"Miss . . . 'Libby' . . . is it?" She sniffed disdainfully. "I carry a message to ye from the milliner and haberdasher of ye olde Camden Harbor Towne. Tonight, as well may ye know, is the festivities and frolicks of a musical entertainment of songs and shanties of the sea. Madam milliner and haberdasher requests that ye stop by her shoppe"—again, pronounced like "shop-pie"—"in order to be outfitted especially for the evening's events, in a frock more befitting of thy general demeanor and the spirit of the evening, as a 'wench,' indeed I believe she said."

Okay. Now time to figure this out. One, I was pretty sure Ashling had just called me a wench, but I'd let that slide. Two, I think I was supposed to stop by the costume shack to pick up something to wear to the Sea Shanty Showdown tonight. I felt like I'd just cracked the Rosetta stone.

Gradually, as I was thinking, Ashling had leaned closer and closer to my cheek, until I finally noticed she was freakishly close.

"Are you examining my pores?" I asked, befuddled.

"I know not what means 'pores.'" She drew back slightly. "Rather that I only suspicioned that one might have bedecked one's complexion with paint as one hears tell of in the brothels and bawdyhouses be seen on ladies of ill repute. One feared that one mayhap had chanced upon a common whore."

Ugh! My jaw dropped, but only for a moment.

"Well, one would really appreciate it if one didn't use language like that in front of the children."

"I know what a 'whore' is," one of the girls piped up. "It's a dental hygienist. Like my dad's girlfriend."

"That actually wasn't what I meant. I was referring to your completely unintelligible syntax, Miss Fennyweather." I mean really, she sounded like Yoda. I wanted my girls to be grammatically correct. "Good day."

I waved her off and returned to the pansies, leaving Miss Fennyweather to shut her parasol briskly and walk, mouth opening and closing like a fish, away down the lane. And the other thing: "Robin, that's not a nice word. I'm sure your dad's girlfriend isn't a whore."

"But my mom *said*."

I dealt with this the rest of our flower-picking excursion, trying not to dissolve into giggles every time my eyes met Cam's, as Cam tried not to choke on his cake, shaking as he was with suppressed laughter. Once the girls had picked enough flowers, they filed inside.

"Hey." Cam straightened and dusted the cake crumbs off his hands, making his way over to me. "I should really get back to the ship. I'll see you at the Showdown tonight. You know where the beach is?"

"Nope." I shook my head.

"Then I'll pick you up outside your ship—the *Lettie Mae,* right?"

"Right." I nodded.

"Sweet." Checking that the girls were inside, he kissed me quickly. "Until tonight," he said, making it sound like a promise—a promise of what, I wasn't sure, but I couldn't wait to find out.

"Tonight." I breathed in the beautiful words, magical *West Side Story* orchestra popping back into my head. "Tonight, tonight, there's only you tonight," I sang softly as I ducked back into the house and Cam hopped the fence.

We had just enough time to get everyone's flowers in the heavy wooden press before two o'clock rolled around and it was drop-off time at the Welcome Center. On my way back, I heard a familiar voice flagging me down.

"Libby! Libby!" I turned. It was Roger, the museum publicist. "It *is* Libby, right?" He caught up with me, wheezing slightly as he placed his hands on his knees to catch his breath.

"Yes, hi, I'm Libby," I introduced myself.

"One of Maddie's interns, right?" I nodded. "I thought so. But I left a message for you with the other one and I had no idea what she was saying, so I wasn't sure if you got it."

"You mean Ash—uh, Susannah Fennyweather?"

"Yeah." I detected the hint of an eye roll. "Did she tell you about the costumes? For the Sea Shanty Showdown?"

"Sort of. I mean, she told me but in her own special way."

"That's what I was afraid of." Definite eye roll. "We've got a pirate wench costume waiting for you down at the shack. I thought we could take some nice publicity shots, for some promotional literature—brochures and stuff—and kind of work the pirate angle. Pirates are fun. People see pirates, they think fun, they think the museum is fun, yadda, yadda, yadda. And the *Camden Crier* is coming to do a piece on it too, so we can get a nice color shot of you in there. You don't mind, right?"

"Um, no, I guess not."

"Thank God." He mopped some sweat off his brow. "I was afraid I wasn't gonna get a wench. The other one wouldn't do it, but she told me 'wenching' would be 'just your cup of tea.'"

Jesus. Thanks, Ashling. "Um, just so you know, Roger, I'm doing this to help the museum, not because I have a particular affinity for 'wenching' or sundry related activities."

"Yep, yep, got it, thanks—you're a doll." He was scanning the town green over my head, looking for someone else. "Thanks a mil. See you at the Showdown." He hurried off.

The costume shack lady was waiting outside the door for me.

"You"—she waved me in excitedly—"are going to *love* this! Saucy with a capital 'S,' missy!" She bulldozed me into the shack and started energetically dressing me.

You know in *Pirates of the Caribbean* when Johnny Depp goes to that tavern in Tortuga, and all the prostitutes slap him? That's what I looked like. Except with less clothing. If I had thought my boobs were out of control in my normal museum gear, they were now practically up to my chin, exploding out of a scarlet satin corset and chemise with two wisps of sleeves. The skirt was ripped and tied up on one side, revealing layers of lacy petticoats, laced-up high-heeled boots, and more leg than had probably ever been seen in the Museum of Maine and the Sea. I felt like I was about to go hawk Captain Morgan rum and wondered if there were any documented cases of spontaneous combustion from embarrassment.

"Aaay!" shrieked the costume lady. "I love it!"

I got the feeling she'd been sort of limited in her costuming options all these years and had quashed a secret desire to design for Vegas showgirls. Or drag queens. She fussed around like a kid in a candy store, pinning up my hair into two messy buns with a bandanna, like a slutty blond pirate Mrs. Lovett from *Sweeney Todd,* and she even busted out an illegal stash of makeup to rouge my cheeks and line my eyes with kohl.

It's all for the good of the museum, I reminded myself over and over again, as I tried unsuccessfully to cover myself up a little bit more. If I had to whore myself out, literally, to save our nation's cultural institutions, then so be it. Future generations would thank me for my sacrifice.

I decided to go hang out onboard the *Lettie Mae* until the Sea Shanty Showdown, as I definitely wasn't leaving the museum grounds dressed like a pirate queen. Plus, ever since Garrett had colonized the ship with his treasure trove of electronic devices, it was officially a cell phone–safe zone. I figured if he had the laptop and the video camera and the voice recorder and God knows what else, one teeny little cell phone more couldn't hurt.

As if my phone could somehow sense that we'd entered neutral territory, the minute I hit the deck, it vibrated.

"Hello?" I answered.

"Libby? Is this Libby? The real Libby?" someone whispered frantically. After a second I recognized Dev's voice.

"Of course it's the real Libby, who else would it be?" I asked quizzically.

"I don't know anymore," he whispered, paranoid. "I don't know anything anymore!"

"Dev, where are you?"

"In a closet." Sniffle. "I never wanted to go back in one, but here I am." Double sniffle.

"Can you speak up? It's really hard to hear you."

"Noooooooooooooooooooooo!" he howled.

"Dev, calm down. Tell me what's going on," I prompted patiently.

"I can't," he said, sobbing quietly. "I can't tell you anything. Libby, I *think they tapped my phone.*" His voice went so low, it was barely audible.

"What? That's ridiculous. Who are 'they,' anyway? Who do you think tapped your phone?"

"Ono-may Orps-cay Ublications-pay."

"What? Who?" I had no idea what he was talking about.

"Mono Corps Publications!" he whisper-screamed. "*Teen Mode's* parent company! Libby, they're *everywhere.*"

"Okay, Dev, you need to calm down and start breathing." I could hear a panic attack coming on over the phone. "Take a few breaths. Nice, long, deep breaths." He took several. "There you go! Good job."

"I did a good job. For once, I did a good job," he said sadly.

"Go to your happy place, Dev. Kelly Clarkson. Happy place. Kelly Clarkson."

"Oh, no, I do not hook up, up, I go slow," he sang softly.

"There you go!" I encouraged him. "Now, whenever you get scared, just sing that song and think of me, and it's like I'm right there with you."

Dev had dubbed Kelly Clarkson's "I Do Not Hook Up" the "Official Libby Kelting Anthem." He took especial delight in singing this whenever we were at parties or dances, as a warning to potential suitors. So maybe I'm a little picky. Sue me. I don't think that's the worst thing in the world.

"Libby," he whispered, "I'm scared."

Click. The line went dead. Yikes. An international publishing conglomerate might have just taken a hit out on my best friend. I tried to call him back several times, but to no avail. Garrett wasn't on the boat, so I paced and thought about Dev until the sun set and it was time for the Showdown. A loud whistle pierced the air. I leaned over the side of the boat; Cam was waiting down on shore, looking up at me. He whistled again. I scurried down the gangplank.

"Damn," Cam said as I hit solid ground. "You look . . ." He was at a loss for words.

"Like a prostitute? I know," I moaned.

"Hot." He shook his head. "I was gonna say hot." He put his arm around me and started steering me toward the boathouse.

"They're making me. The museum. I swear to God, I did not pick this outfit. Roger thinks pirates are 'fun' and wants to put pirate pictures in the *Camden Crier*. He thinks it'll make more people come to the museum."

"It'd certainly make me come." He smirked.

"So where are we going?" I changed topics quickly, blushing. If I was gonna keep hanging out with Cam, I needed to stop embarrassing so easily.

"The beach. Not the town beach, the museum beach. It's that smallish strip of sand next to the boathouse. There, you see? Where the bonfire is."

I did. It was glowing in the distance, shooting orange sparks into the darkening dusk. As night fell, the sky deepened to a shade of blue that was almost navy, dark enough to see the first stars of evening twinkling above.

The boathouse was a large wooden structure on the dock, with three walls and one side open to the beach. We walked down the length of the dock and entered the boathouse from the side, through propped-open double doors that looked like they fell off the side of a barn. Directly inside, there was a pirate at a desk with a series of lists.

"Ahoy." The pirate waved. "Be ye checkin' in and competin' in the Showdown, arrgggh?"

"You look like a tool." Cam chuckled.

"Dude, shut up," the pirate said. "They forced me to wear this."

"This" was a cobbled-together pirate outfit clearly meant to channel Jack Sparrow, except the sashes around his head and waist were a Barbie hot pink. The black dread-locked wig and beard he had on were threatening to consume his head altogether. He was drowning in a sea of nylon dreadlocks. I assumed the pirate had applied his own eyeliner, or else a six-year-old had sloppily drawn circles around his eyes with a black crayon. He looked like a mangy panda's piratical cousin.

"I feel your pain," I sympathized.

"Well, you look hot," the pirate grumped. "I look like a tool."

"You look very . . . distinguished," I offered.

"Be ye singing, wench?" he asked, waving around a ball-point pen with a giant feathery plume taped to it.

"Hells no," I said firmly. I would prance around all tarted

up, but that was the extent of the humiliation I was willing to endure in the name of history. Nobody needed to hear me mangle a shanty.

"Cam, you doing anything solo or just the annual Squaddie 'What Do You Do with a Drunken Sailor?'?" the pirate asked, list in hand.

"Just 'Drunken Sailor.'"

The pirate checked something off.

I looked around while Cam and the pirate, who turned out to also be on the Demo Squad, talked. The walls had been decorated with all types of different pirate flags; not just the skull and crossbones Jolly Roger, but the skull and cutlasses, bleeding hearts, little devils, and skeletons. The band was in the back center of the room—fiddle, accordion, banjo, and fife—already playing merrily away. Sea shanties were actually pretty catchy; my toe was involuntarily tapping, and I felt the unfamiliar urge to start jigging or something.

There were a lot of faces, and a few I recognized. Ashling was there, in Susannah Fennyweather garb, dutifully studying some sheet music. Suze stood next to her, looking absolutely miserable in a pirate costume, trying to stabilize the stuffed parrot that kept threatening to pitch off her shoulder. Neil and the marine biologists stood just off to the side of the boathouse in the sand, clinking beer bottles together. Neil was still bandaged but looked to be enjoying himself immensely.

Garrett was standing in the corner of the boathouse, looking awkward and slightly defeated. I had a feeling I knew why. There hadn't been the merest hint of paranormal activity onboard the *Lettie Mae*. As a kind of summer opener, he'd published an article summing up all the earlier ghost sightings, but I knew he wasn't happy with it.

"Come on, Libs. Let's go get a beer before all the good stuff's gone." Cam put his arm around my waist and pulled me away from the pirate table.

"Oh, um, I'm not twenty-one," I said as we walked out to the beach.

"Ah, but I am." He winked. Wow. I had guessed that Cam was a little older than me, but I hadn't realized he was twenty-one! That was so . . . mature. I knew it was kind of silly, but I couldn't help but feel cool that someone older was interested in me. I mean, Cam probably could have gone to the Showdown with anyone, and he'd picked *me*. Me! There were two large barrels full of ice just outside. He pulled two beers out of one of the barrels and popped them open with a bottle opener on his key chain. "And here you are, m'lady." He handed one to me, executing a joking half-bow and winking again.

"Oh, thank you, but I don't really like beer. I—" Cam had taken a deep swig and wasn't paying any attention. I took a small sip and made a face. Ugh. Beer is just gross. Even the smell—yuck.

Cam started chugging his beer, as a group of guys walked over.

"Yo, Cam!" Ah. Squaddies. They all started talking, drinking, and laughing, in a maelstrom of *man*s and *bro*s, and Cam promptly forgot all about me. I looked in the other barrel. Root beer. I wondered . . . I held my beer bottle up. The two were almost identical. I hid my beer in the sand behind the barrel and exchanged it for a root beer, which luckily had a twist-off top. I took a long, sweet gulp. Much better.

"Babe? Babe! Hey, babe!" Bro-fest was over, apparently.

"Yeah, Cam?" I trotted over, trying not to topple over in the uneven sand in my silly little boots.

"Babe, these are my boys," he introduced me. They all stared directly at my chest. I bet not one of them would have been able to recognize my face if we met up later.

"Hi." I blushed. I swore one day to wreak vengeance on Roger for this outfit.

"Kelly!" one said excitedly.

"What?" I asked, confused. "No, um, I'm—"

"Melissa?" another one asked.

"No, I'm Libby." I shot Cam a quizzical look.

"Libs, we've gotta go practice, okay?" He kissed me sloppily, and it tasted like beer. "We'll be back. Don't miss me too much."

"Damn, son, how do you do it?!" one yelled as the pack of them walked off. "You are a legend, Cam-man!" They high-fived and laughed, leaving me with a sinking feeling in the pit of my stomach, and I wondered who exactly Kelly and Melissa were.

I was alone in the sand, in the darkness, watching the bonfire shoot up into the now black night sky. I could've gone to talk to Neil and the marine biologists, but I was starting to feel like there was some kind of weird love triangle going on. And as badly as I wanted to rescue Suze and her floppy parrot, I really didn't think I could face Ashling in my historical hooker gear.

"Hey."

It was Garrett, fiddling awkwardly with his voice recorder.

"This is Janine." He stepped aside to reveal a short woman

with a camera. I always forgot that Garrett was actually quite tall—not Neil tall but still really tall, taller than Cam, surprisingly. He hunched a little, like he wasn't totally comfortable with how tall he was. "She's the, um, photographer at the *Camden Crier*. Do you mind if she takes your picture?"

"Oh, uh, no, of course not." We stepped into better light, closer to the boathouse.

"She's going to be running around doing candids mostly, but they want a few stills too," he explained, as Janine gave us the thumbs-up, indicating the light was good.

"Here." I gave him my bottle. "Would you hold my root beer? It looks like real beer, and I feel like that's not exactly the family-friendly image the museum should project."

"I, uh, don't know that your, um, outfit is exactly a family-friendly image."

He was clearly exerting superhuman effort not to look at my chest.

"It's okay." I sighed. "You can look. They're sort of hard to avoid."

"I have no idea what you're talking about." He studiously looked up and away, looked anywhere that wasn't directly down my shirt.

"You're a good guy, Garrett."

"You don't need to sound quite so surprised, Libby." He grinned sheepishly.

"I mean, don't get me wrong, you're still a jerk. And a weird-o," I clarified, "but there may be hope for you yet."

"Uh, thanks, I guess." He pushed his glasses up on his nose, like he was embarrassed or something.

I smiled, and Janine took my picture, before moving back into the boathouse, leaving me and Garrett standing alone in the moonlit sand.

"So, how are you enjoying your first Sea Shanty Showdown?" he asked, breaking the silence.

"Off the record? Or is this in your official capacity as *Camden Crier* reporter?" I asked.

"Off the record," he said. "Libby Kelting, uncut and uncensored."

"It's . . . fine, I guess."

"Fine? That sounded pretty censored." He laughed.

"Okay, okay, umm, let's see," I began. "I like the music. More than I thought I would. And the actual Showdown hasn't even started yet, so it'll probably only get better. So that's a plus. And this root beer is delicious." I took my bottle back. "But I saw Ashling with some sheet music, and that makes me very apprehensive."

"That does sound scary," he agreed. "So . . . where's your boyfriend?"

"He's not my boyfriend." I looked down at the sand. "But if you mean Cam, he went to go practice with the other Squaddies."

"Ah, yes, the annual Demo Squad serenade of 'What Do You Do with a Drunken Sailor?' in which they all try to outdo each other in emulating the titular sailor," he said disdainfully.

"Ahoy!" We turned simultaneously toward the boathouse, where President Harrow was standing in front of the band, microphone in hand. "Ahoy, avast, and gather ye round, mateys!"

President Harrow was also in full pirate regalia and looked like he was having the time of his life.

Garrett and I followed everyone else into the boathouse.

"Welcome to the Sea Shanty Showdown, laddies and lassies!" he continued, booming over the microphone. "I be Captain Harrow, and welcome to me boathouse. The Dread Pirate Travis"—President Harrow indicated the unhappy-looking pirate who had signed us in—"will be announcin' the competitors as they take the stage. When it be over, the dread panel of judges, who be me-self, the Jolly Roger"—here he indicated Roger the publicist—"and sweet Maddie May"—our internship coordinator, in a black pantsuit and an eye patch—"will be pickin' the top three, and then ye, the unruly mob, shall decide the victor by the ancient test of the sea: the applause-o-meter!" The crowd cheered. "Dread Pirate Travis, the mike be yours. ARRRGH!" President Harrow finished up and passed the mike.

"Hey," Travis said glumly in the microphone. "Ashling? Did I pronounce that right? Ashling? Whatever."

"IT IS SUSANNAH FENNYWEATHER!" she boomed, roughly snatching the microphone away from Travis. "I know not what be this volume-enhancing stick of sorcery, but use it I shall."

Someone who sounded like Cam snickered and repeated, "Stick of sorcery." I turned—all the Squaddies were in the back of the boathouse, clinking bottles and chugging beer.

Ashling then busted out an off-key, operatic rendition of something called "Yankee Privateer," which lasted for the longest seven minutes of my life. Yes, seven whole minutes. I watched them tick slooowly away on Garrett's watch.

Once Ashling quit the stage, amid a halfhearted smattering of applause, things improved vastly. Lots of different people and groups from the museum got up to sing, most of whom I didn't know, singing songs I didn't recognize, but they were all really good. I even found myself dancing a little bit to "Maggie May." The Squaddies went last, and by this point they were all so trashed that "What Do You Do with a Drunken Sailor?" was almost unintelligible. They swayed together in a large clump, until the one on the end abruptly fell over and passed out, cutting the song short with a dramatic conclusion. Laughing raucously, they dragged their fallen comrade offstage, back into the corner closest to the beer.

"Now is the time for anyone who has been inspired by the magic of music and the spirit of the sea to sing if they so choose," the Dread Pirate Travis read dispassionately off a sheet of paper, returning to his post on the microphone.

"Libby does a unique interpretation of 'Hey, Ho, Blow the Man Down,'" Ashling said nastily, putting extra emphasis on the words *ho* and *blow*.

"Yeah, Libby, blow the man down!" one of the Squaddies yelled.

"Cam, dude, you *need* to hit that," another Squaddie said, so loudly and drunkenly that everyone heard.

"Are you singing 'Blow the Man Down'?" Travis pointed the microphone limply in my direction.

"NO!" I shouted, trying not to cry, although my lip betrayed me with a telltale wobble. I felt someone touch my arm. It was Garrett, and he looked pissed, a muscle tightening in his jaw.

"Are you okay?" he asked concernedly. "Don't pay any attention to them," he whispered. "They're just drunk assholes."

"I know," I whispered back. If I cried at something called a Sea Shanty Showdown, I would never forgive myself.

"Okay, then. Whatever," Travis continued, "are you gonna sing something else?"

"Um . . ."

"Sing! Sing! Sing!" Somehow, a drunken chant/slow clap had materialized. "Do it! Do it!"

It was like a mob situation. People I didn't know were propelling me forward, until I somehow, inexplicably, ended up in front of the band, microphone in hand, abandoned by the Dread Pirate Travis. Garrett stood in the corner, shrugging wildly, making facial movements like he was sorry but had no idea what had happened.

I didn't know any sea shanties. I mean, yes, I had recognized the tune of a *few* of them from Ashling's CD, but that's it. I didn't know any of the lyrics. Standing up in front of a packed boathouse, I could only think of one vaguely water-related song I knew all the words to, because Dev had preformed it as Tina Turner in the talent portion of the Miss Gay Minnesota Drag Pageant, and I had been one of his backup dancers. It wasn't a sea shanty. It was a body-of-water pop song. But it was the best I had.

"Do you guys know 'Proud Mary'?" I turned to the band. Silence. "Tina Turner?" I whispered frantically. Nothing. Oh, this was not good. "Just, um, follow my lead, I guess." That worked in movies and stuff.

"I left a good job in the city," I started tentatively, a cappella.

"Working for the man every night and day

And I never lost one minute of sleeping
Worrying 'bout the way things might have been."

The accordion player picked up on what I was doing.

"Big wheel keep on turning
Proud Mary keep on burning."

Now the whole band was in on it—fiddle, accordion, banjo, and all.

"And we're rolling, rolling
Rolling on the river."

Now I was really getting into it. Like full-on belting it out, and the band was rocking. Well, as much as an accordion can rock.

"Cleaned a lot of plates in Memphis
Pumped a lot of 'tane down in New Orleans
But I never saw the good side of the city
Till I hitched a ride on a riverboat queen."

Without me even knowing that I was doing it, I'd started up the arm motions. The original choreography had arisen from the depths of my subconscious and it was out in full force.

"Big wheel keep on turning
Proud Mary keep on burning
And we're rolling, I said we're rolling
Rolling on the river."

By this point, the crowd was really into it. Like jumping and screaming and *wooh*ing and singing along. People were even dancing! I felt like frickin' eighteenth-century pirate Hannah Montana or something, with all those screaming people.

> "If you come down to the river
> I bet you gonna find some people who live
> You don't have to worry if you got no money
> People on the river are happy to give."

Yeah, I was full-on Tina Turner–ing it up there. Like crazy-dancing power-belting Tina Turner.

> "Big wheel keep on turning
> Proud Mary keep on burning
> And we're rolling, rolling
> Rolling on the river."

People were *wooh*ing and calling, "Take it home! Wooh! Yeow!" And I did.

> "Rolling, yeah! Rolling, rolling on the river.
> Rolling, ooh! Rolling, rolling on the river.
> Rolling, rolling, rolling on the river."

The crowd erupted into thunderous applause. All of sudden, I remembered where I was, blushed furiously, and shoved the microphone back at Travis. It was like I'd been momentarily possessed by Tina Turner, and she'd just left my body.

"What," Garrett shouted over the roar, clapping madly, "the hell was that?!"

"I have no idea!" I shouted back.

"That was amazing! I had no idea you could sing like that!"

"Oh, I was in church choir, back in Minnesota, and stuff."

"Church choir." He laughed. "Jesus, Libby, that was something else."

"Quiet, quiet." Travis was tapping the microphone, restoring order. "The judges have determined that, although that was face-meltingly awesome, it was not, in fact, a shanty, so disqualified. Bummer."

A handful of people booed, but I didn't care about winning the Showdown. He proceeded to announce the three finalists. I clapped distractedly throughout the applause-o-meter, barely noticing that my favorite "Maggie May" group took first place —I was too jittery from all the adrenaline. It was like I'd just chugged a case of Diet Coke, eaten a bag of Pixy Stix, and gone on a roller coaster. As the crowd broke up, I went out to get a root beer for the way home.

When I got back in, I looked around for Cam—we had come together, so I had thought we would leave together. But the only Squaddie I saw was the one who had passed out, who was now awake and vomiting noisily into a pirate hat.

I left the boathouse and stood on the dock, scanning the beach and the water for Cam.

"Libby, he's not coming." It was Garrett, standing behind me, fiddling awkwardly with the zipper on his navy hoodie sweatshirt.

"Well, he might." Garrett gave me a look. "Okay, he's probably not coming," I agreed, "but we didn't make plans to leave together or anything, so —"

"You can't apologize for him forever," Garrett said sanctimoniously.

"That's none of your business," I snapped. God, why did he always act like he was better than everybody?

"Sorry." He sounded surprised. "I was just trying to —"

"Well, stop. Just stop." I hugged myself, cold in the wind. I sighed noisily, not really in the mood to fight. "It's been a long night."

"No kidding." He ran a hand though his messy hair. "Especially when Ashling sang 'Yankee Privateer.'"

I laughed shakily. "True story. I think I aged seven years in those seven minutes." I shivered even more violently. Even though it was summer, it got cold at night.

"Come on." He started walking. "Let's go home."

"You know," I said, as I trotted after him with my teeth starting to chatter. "This would be the point where a gentleman would offer me his coat." Because even though it said "Starfleet Academy" on the back of his hoodie, I was cold enough that even that was looking appealing.

"I didn't think you'd want it." He shrugged. "It doesn't go with your outfit."

"Wow, Garrett." I was stunned. "I didn't know one could manage to be both sensitive and insensitive at the same time."

"It's a gift," he said, stopping to unzip his hoodie. He held it out to me. "Are you coming?"

Wordlessly, I took the hoodie from his outstretched hand, and followed him into the night.

chapter six

"Please just put on the SPF forty-five."

"No, Suze, no! For the thousandth time, no!" I sat up in my *Little Mermaid* beach chair and turned to look at her. "I want to come back from this summer at least a little tan."

"You'll be very sorry if you come back with even a little skin cancer." She squirted out another giant blob of sunscreen. I don't know where she kept putting it, as there was barely a square inch of her flesh exposed to the sun. She had on a huge straw hat, sunglasses, an oversize "Go Public!" NPR T-shirt, and capris over her bathing suit. I hadn't actually seen said alleged bathing suit, but I assumed it was pretty full coverage.

"I'm not gonna get skin cancer!" I shuffled around in my beach bag and pulled out the Hawaiian Tropic bottle I'd just bought at the CVS. "See? This Golden Tanning Lotion has SPF six!"

She shook her head. "Libby, I'm just saying, there's no need to give you-know-who more ammo. She's really, really mad."

"What? Who?" I reclined my chair, closing my eyes under my sunglasses. "Ashling?"

"Yes," she whispered, looking over her shoulder to peer under the nearby beach umbrellas.

I don't know what she was looking for—even though we were at the public beach in downtown Camden Harbor, at the height of tourist season, there was barely anyone there. Just a mom with two little kids, and another girl around our age, napping in the sun in an itsy-bitsy bikini.

"You don't need to call her you-know-who, Suze. We're not in *Harry Potter,* and she's not Voldemort. Fear of name creates fear of a thing. Or whatever it was that Dumbledore said."

"Fine. *Ashling* is really, really mad."

"What's she mad about?" I asked.

"The Sea Shanty Showdown!" Suze squealed. "She is furious, *furious,* that you didn't perform an actual shanty. She's been yelling about historical accuracy and total disrespect for traditions and all sorts of things nonstop. And then last night I heard someone screaming in the basement . . . screaming like a wounded animal." Suze's eyes took on a haunted look. "For a brief, crazy second, I thought it was the ghost, but then I noticed Ashling wasn't in her bed. She won't admit it, but I think she's also really mad that you got more applause than she did. Which is probably why she resorted to primal-scream therapy, to try to deal with these feelings she can't express or articulate, because she's trying to deny them," Suze added thoughtfully.

"Yikes." It's not like I had gone out of my way to piss Ashling off. I hadn't even planned on singing. Really, she had no one to blame but herself—she started it. I never would have even been up there in the first place without her catalytic "Blow the Man Down" comment. "So she's really mad, huh?" I chewed my lip.

"Yes. And then when I asked her if she wanted to come to the beach with us—"

"You asked her if she wanted to come to the beach with us?!" I shot back up. "Suze, it's my day off. I want to *enjoy* myself."

To that end, I'd invited Suze to pick up beach supplies (magazines, tanning lotion, foldable Disney-printed children's beach chairs, and towels) at the CVS in downtown Camden Harbor and walk to the beach with me to spend the afternoon in the sun. I reasoned it would be silly to spend a whole summer on the Maine coast and never have seen the beach.

"I know, I know," she apologized. "But I didn't want to leave her out. I didn't want to make things worse than they already are. I wanted to make peace."

"To use a nautical phrase, I think that ship has sailed." I leaned back again.

"But then she went on this diatribe about needing to protect her porcelain complexion from the sun's fierce power," Suze continued in a rush, "and how only a—oh, what did she say —a 'common streetwalking slag,'" Suze remembered, "would allow herself to be browned by the sun."

"Gee, I wonder who she was talking about," I said sarcastically.

"Libby, what if she stones you? Or builds stocks and a pillory in the town green? Or makes you wear a scarlet letter?" Suze asked fearfully.

"While I wouldn't put any of those past her, I think I'll be okay. Ashling doesn't run Camden Harbor. What is she going to do, ask Maddie to have the costume shack embroider a scarlet 'T' for 'tan' on my chest?" Plus, that kind of punishment had gone out with the Puritans in the 1600s. It was 1791 in Camden Harbor—practically the modern age. Ashling would never do something so historically inaccurate.

Suze picked up her book. I rustled around in my bag and pulled out my *Martha Stewart Living*. Thankfully, it was *not* owned by Mono Corps, which I'd decided to boycott as a sign of solidarity with my still absent friend. I hadn't heard from Dev since that last frightening conversation, and I was starting to think it increasingly likely that he'd been whacked by the cashmere mafia. And no matter what I did, no matter how many times I called him, I couldn't reach him! It was so frustrating to know that something was wrong but not be able to do anything about it.

I flipped it open: "Martha's Flower-Arranging Secrets: Six Steps to Beautiful Bouquets." Ah, now this was more like it. Relaxing in the sunshine with a lovely floral pictorial spread. I was well on my way to a beautiful bouquet—five steps in, in fact—when . . .

"Hey."

I looked up, squinting into the sun in my cheap white designer-knockoff sunglasses. They sort of made me look like a bug, but I liked them. I held up a hand to shield my eyes and saw Garrett standing above me, illuminated by the sun.

"Hey, Garrett, what's up?" I squinted at him. We'd been getting along a lot better since the Sea Shanty Showdown. I'd learned not to bring up anything that could possibly prompt him to wax rhapsodic about sci-fi or computer games or anything equally lame, and he'd learned not to walk around barefoot. He'd even stopped calling me "Hello Kitty" for the most part. Sometimes he called me "Proud Mary" now, but I decided that was an upgrade.

"Do you know Suze?" I asked. They nodded at each other. It seemed like Garrett knew everybody here, but I guess he was actually *from* Camden Harbor, so it made sense. Plus he had all those nosy investigative reporter instincts.

"Hi," she said shyly, squirting out an extra-big goop of still-more SPF 45.

"You here to work on the tan?" I asked him. "Because no offense, you've got a long way to go." I mean, Garrett almost made me look tan, and I was one step away from albino. But nothing creates a pallor like bathing yourself in the flicker of a computer screen. Turned out I'd been right about my World of Warcraft hunch. Garrett had confessed one night that he'd had to quit cold turkey after he'd been so involved with the game, he almost missed his own graduation.

"No, definitely not here to tan." He laughed. "I use my extreme farmer's tan to distract the opposing side when we play shirts versus skins in Ultimate Frisbee. I can't lose that competitive edge." I snorted. "I'm going kayaking. With Neil."

Garrett pointed to the shoreline, where Neil was sitting in a yellow two-seater kayak. I waved at Neil, who waved giddily back with his good arm.

"Wait, how can Neil kayak?" I realized there was something wrong with that picture. "He's still all bandaged up and stuff. He can't use his shoulder or arm or anything. And I'm not a kayak expert, but I'm pretty sure you need your arms. And shoulders."

"Yes, both are important," Garrett agreed. "But I ran into him the other day, and he was so bummed about not being able to kayak—it was one of the main reasons he wanted to film the documentary here—I offered to take him out in a kayak and paddle him around. I mean, it's not the same, obviously," he said, shrugging, "but I figured it was better than nothing."

Would that even be physically possible? It's not like Garrett was a super jock. I mean, obviously. But then I looked at his arms. He actually had much nicer arms than I would have thought, arms that definitely looked like they could paddle around the world's tallest documentary filmmaker.

"Wow. That's really nice of you, Garrett," I said.

"Oh, I don't mind." He shrugged again. "I like kayaking."

"I've never gone."

"Well, you should!" His eyes lit up. "If you want, sometime, we could—"

"Hey."

Suze squeaked. Cam was standing on the opposite side of my beach chair, across from Garrett, miles of tanned torso shining in the sun above a low-slung plaid Abercrombie bathing suit.

"Hey, Libs." Cam reached down to tousle my hair, which was continuing its curling summer trend and currently threatening to explode from the ponytail holder I'd casually tossed it up in. "Hey, man, what's up," he said, nodding nonchalantly at Garrett.

"Not much," Garrett replied tersely, clenching his jaw. "Bye, Libby. Suze." He turned and abruptly left in the direction of Neil and the big yellow kayak.

"Someone's got an extra-big stick up his ass today." Cam snickered.

"Hmm," I said dryly, and straightened my sunglasses on my nose. To be perfectly honest, at the moment I wasn't all that happy with Cam either.

"Aw, come on, babe, not you too," he groaned.

Not-me-too what? Not-me-too with a stick up my ass? Great. Thanks. I snippily flipped a page of *Martha*.

"Aw, Libs, you're not upset about the Showdown, are you?"

Flip. Flip. Flip.

Truth be told, I *was* a little upset about the sea shanty shambles. Cam had gotten trashed, completely ditched me, let his friends basically call me a slut in front of the whole museum, and to top it all off, he'd missed my "Proud Mary" moment of glory.

"You know I wanted to spend more time with you. I'd be crazy not to want to spend every minute with you." He grinned. "But I had to leave. Scrubs was so wasted, I needed to take him home."

Scrubs? Was that a person? What the hell kind of name was that? Flip.

"Come on, Libs, you know how it is. Scrubs is my boy. I couldn't leave him hurting like that."

Flip. Flip.

"Okay, I think I know what you're really mad about." He sighed heavily. For some weird reason, he darted a nervous glance over to the shoreline, where the napping girl and the family were. After a quick look, he turned back to me and sunk to his knees, crouching by my chair. "Libby, I'm really, really sorry about my friends. Some of the things they said were way out of line. They're really not that bad. My friends are just assholes when they drink. And I know that doesn't excuse their behavior, and I should've said something, but they're my friends, you know? It's complicated."

I looked at him for the first time, and he really did look truly, deeply sorry. I was falling into those gray-blue eyes, unable to tear myself away.

"Please, Libby. Please say you'll forgive me. I am so, so sorry," he said sincerely. "Let me make it up to you."

"Well," I hemmed and hawed. God, I just couldn't say no to him! He was just too cute. "What did you have in mind?" I conceded, and immediately a beatific grin broke out across his impossibly handsome face, like the sun bursting through rain clouds.

"I wanna take you out on my boat," he said excitedly. "Come on, babe, you'll love it. It'll be really fun. And romantic, out there on the water." He smiled devastatingly. "Just say yes."

Oh, I wanted to. I really, really wanted to—more than I should have.

"But . . . Suze," I protested halfheartedly. "I shouldn't leave her."

"Aw, she doesn't mind. Am I right, sweetheart?" He turned the full force of his charms on to Suze, who stopped breathing.

"Suze?" I poked her to make sure she was still alive.

"Go. Libby. Go," she said in three little gasping breaths.

"Then it's settled." He stood, pulling me up with him. Out of the corner of my eye, I noticed the napping girl sit up. "Come on, come on, let's go," Cam said, strangely urgent. I grabbed my beach bag, stuffing in my magazine, *Pocahontas* beach towel, and the denim cutoffs I'd worn over my navy and white polka dot bikini as Cam dragged me away and I skidded along the sand in my striped flip-flops.

The Camden Harbor Town Marina was just adjacent to the public beach, mere steps off the sand and down the dock to Cam's boat slip. For someone working at a maritime history museum, I was appallingly ignorant when it came to sailing, boats, and all that jazz. What's worse, I had no real desire to be better informed. Whenever the conversation turned to boats, I completely, instantaneously, zoned out. Like people might as well be speaking Farsi. So as Cam waxed rhapsodic about his "nineteen-foot gaff-rigged wooden lapstrake daysailer sloop with outboard sails and boom tent," I knew all I'd remember was that the boat was white and cute.

It really was very pretty, with white wooden sides and a gleaming dark wood interior. As I climbed in and settled myself into the tiny bench seating area, I couldn't help but notice that the boat was in flawless condition—impeccably maintained. Cam clearly lavished a lot of love and attention on it.

"Welcome aboard," he said proudly. "Babe, meet my baby."

"What's she called?" Boats were *she*s. That I did know.

"Fanny Hill."

"Like the titular prostitute in the eighteenth-century erotic novel?"

"Ummm . . . yeah." He looked really surprised. "You're smart, for a girl. People don't usually get that."

"History nerd." I shrugged, choosing to let that "for a girl" comment slide.

"Right." He looked oddly disconcerted and immediately started busying himself with whatever business it took to make a boat actually sail.

There was a good breeze, and before I knew it, the marina was disappearing into the distance, becoming a smaller and smaller speck of brown against the beach. Sailing was fun! We were flying along the water. I stuck my head over the side, straight into the wind, totally heedless of whatever madness was sure to be wreaked upon my hair.

"I love this!" I called to Cam over the roar of the wind. He flashed me a smile and a double thumbs-up. It was too windy to really talk, and Cam was busy tacking the jib boom or something most of the time, so I just enjoyed the wind and the sea and the waves and the sky. We blew past a chain of little islands and an old lighthouse. I wondered if there was a feisty codger with a shotgun inside.

It felt like only minutes, but it must have been much later when Cam expertly navigated us into a small cove in one of the islands, as the sun was starting to set.

"Oh, how beautiful," I said with a sigh, as the sky turned pink.

Cam finished whatever he was doing and came to join me on the bench.

"Beautiful? Next to you, the sunset could never compare." He gazed deeply into my eyes and recited:

"Shall I compare thee to a summer's day?
Thou art more lovely and more temperate.
Rough winds do shake the darling buds of May,
And summer's lease hath all too short a date."

Oh my God. It was like a movie. But better. Because it was *real.* He leaned closer and pushed an errant strand of hair out of my eyes. His hand lingered on my cheek.

"Sometime too hot the eye of heaven shines,
And often is his gold complexion dimmed;
And every fair from fair sometime declines,
By chance or nature's changing course untrimmed.
But thy eternal summer shall not fade—"

BZZZZZ. BZZZZZ.

Cam leaned back slightly, startled. "Are your boobs vibrating? Or are you just happy to see me?" he cracked, laughing at his own joke.

"That joke doesn't make any sense." I wrinkled my nose. "I—oh—right! Boobs! Vibrating! Phone!" I'd gotten used to keeping my phone in my bra. It was really convenient. So I'd stashed my phone in one triangle of my bikini top before I'd left the *Lettie Mae* and promptly forgot it was in there. Scrambling away from Cam to have enough room to maneuver my elbows, I extracted the phone. Dev! I hurriedly slid it open.

"Dev! Dev! Are you okay?!"

All I could hear was crying. Huge, racking, gut-wrenching sobs. And then the phone went dead. I held it up. No service.

"Nooooo!" I shouted, waving it around over my head, looking for reception.

"Libs, what's going on?" Cam was trying to get a comforting arm around my shoulder, but I was still doing a service-searching flail.

"It's my friend Dev," I explained, slightly hysterical. "He's doing this awful, scary internship at a teen fashion magazine, and he was crying, which means he's either really upset or Meryl Streep just *killed* him."

"Uh . . . okay." He stared at me blankly.

"Either way, I need to get back to land and talk to him *now*."

"What do you mean, get back to land?" Now he just looked confused.

"I need to get back where there's service. My friend is really upset. Or in trouble."

"But . . . but we were gonna watch the sunset," he said in a tone that suggested we weren't going to be watching anything.

"I—I know," I stammered, "but my friend—"

"I'm sure your friend is fine," he whispered soothingly, stroking my arm with one hand and maneuvering the other one around my waist. "Don't worry. Don't think about him. Think about us." He leaned in. "Here. Now. Together."

"Cam." I pulled back as he leaned in to kiss me. "Seriously. Please take me back to shore. Now." I had never heard Dev cry like that, and I needed to be in a place where I could be there for him.

"Come on, Libs, seriously?" Cam looked like he didn't believe me.

"Seriously. Cam. Take me home."

"Fine," he snapped, sighing with frustration and pouting like a kid who'd just been told he wasn't going to Toys "R" Us.

The ride back to the marina was chilly—and not because of the setting sun. Cam maintained a frosty silence the whole way back.

"Thank you, Cam, for taking me out on your boat," I said as I hopped out on the dock. "I had a nice time."

"Well, I'm glad one of us did," he muttered. "Thanks for showing your appreciation. I could tell you were really grateful."

I stared at him, shocked. I'd never heard that tone in his voice. But immediately the ugly look on his face melted away into the sincerest contrition.

"God, Libs, I am so sorry," he apologized. "I was just upset that we didn't get to spend more time together." He smiled sheepishly. "I just want to be selfish and keep you all to myself. Forgive me?" Cam stuck his hands in his pockets and looked shyly down at me.

"Of—of course." I leaned up and kissed his cheek, somewhat warily. "Now, I really have to go—"

"Of course, of course, go call your friend." He shooed me onward. "Go!"

I waved and jogged away over the sand back towards the museum. I dialed Dev nonstop the entire walk back to the museum, but I never reached him. Aargh! I was furious with myself for missing his call. How many times had Dev been there for me, and now, when it was my turn to be there for him, I was gadding about in a sailboat! I was the worst friend ever.

Garrett was standing on deck, watching the sun dip into the water, munching contemplatively on handfuls of Froot Loops he pulled out of a giant cereal box.

"How was your day?" he asked, eyes still on the sunset.

"Not the best," I admitted.

Garrett's face lit up like a Christmas tree. "I'd say I'm sorry, but I'm not, really. I'm hardly surprised."

"*Mmmm.*" I decided not to press him for an explanation but instead reached for a handful of Froot Loops.

Together, we munched our way through the cereal box, watching as the ocean swallowed the sun and night fell.

"Well, I guess I'd better get ghost hunting. Not that there seems to be much point," he added dejectedly.

"Can I stake out with you?" I asked, on a whim.

"Really?" His eyebrows rose above his glasses in surprise. "You want to stay up with me and watch for the ghost?"

"Yeah, why not." I shrugged. "It might be fun. And I'm getting bored just hanging out in the fo'c's'le reading in the dark."

"Well, yeah, okay. I guess so."

"I promise not to do anything even remotely Nancy Drew," I said seriously. "No old clocks, no hidden staircases, no mysterious letters, nothing."

"Then it's a deal." He grinned.

We headed down to the fo'c's'le to grab our camping lanterns.

"Frank was the brunette, and Joe was the blonde, right?" I wondered out loud, only semiconscious that I was speaking.

"Frank and Joe who?" Garrett handed me my lantern.

"Hardy." I took it and flipped it to its brightest setting.

"Nancy, what did we just talk about?" he warned.

"Right. Gotcha. Jinkies." That was Scooby-Doo, which was a whole other set of teenage detectives, so I reasoned it was fair game. Garrett shot me an exaggerated glare but didn't say anything.

"You ready?"

"I was born ready." I followed Garrett's retreating back deeper into the belly of the ship. "Where, um, are we going?" I picked my way carefully over the uneven wooden planks.

"The galley. Which is the kitchen-slash-dining area of the ship."

"I know what a galley is!" I protested. "I'm not *that* nautically impaired."

"Just making sure," he said, turning a corner.

"I'm really not as stupid as you think I am," I muttered.

"I don't think you're stupid," he said, surprise audible in his voice.

"Well, that's news to me," I muttered again. "But you did, didn't you?" I challenged him.

"I will admit I may have . . . underestimated you," he said grudgingly. Victory!

"Wow, did the infallible Garrett McCaffrey just admit he was *wrong* about something?" I teased.

"Hardly. I admitted to a miscalculation, not an error." He sounded like his smug old self, but there was a little something in his voice that made think that if I could have seen him, he would have been smiling.

God, it was dark and creepy in there. I really, really didn't like it. The boat rocked very gently from side to side, causing the ropes and lanterns that swung from the ceiling to cast shifting shadows along the sloping walls. The camping lantern could barely keep the oppressive blackness at bay. I couldn't imagine how Garrett did this all alone night after night. I would have peed myself or something. "Here we are."

The galley itself was a tiny room crammed with kitchen supplies that opened into the biggest room I'd seen so far on the *Lettie Mae*. It had a long wooden table flanked by wooden benches, all nailed to the floor. Tin mugs and plates were set all the way down it, and barrels lined the walls.

"Every time there's been a sighting, the ghost has been spotted at the other end of the dining area," Garrett continued. "So I've been hunkering down in the galley, sort of hiding behind these fake sacks of cornmeal."

"Sounds like a plan." I stepped into the galley and over a few sacks. "Is there any way we could maybe construct a slightly larger, harder-to-penetrate barrier using more sacks?"

"Libby, the sacks aren't for protection; they're so we remain unobserved," he said, joining me in the galley. "You're not . . . afraid of the ghost, are you?" he asked curiously.

"What! Um, no! Obviously not!" I denied it a little too ve-hemently. Now that Garrett had finally admitted he'd underes-timated me, I didn't want to lose my newfound cred. "I don't know what you're talking about. I am not scared at all. At all. Not at all. Nope. No sirree, Bob." I shook my head.

"I'll get you an extra sack of cornmeal." He dragged one over and added it to the pile.

"Danger is my middle name," I was still babbling. "Libby Danger Kelting. So bring it on. Bring it on, ghostie. Ghostie ghostie ghost ghost. Ghostface. Ghostface Killah."

"Um, what is going on? Do you have a crack problem I don't know about?" He flicked off both of our lamps, plunging us into complete darkness.

"High on life, Garrett. High on life."

More like high on crazy-adrenaline-fear-rush. Why was I being such a baby? There was no such thing as ghosts. I mean I knew that, obviously. But way down there in the darkness, trapped in the depths of the ship with no easy way out, it was really, really scary. I scooted a little closer to Garrett and hoped he didn't notice. Not that it was going to help, because I seri-ously doubted Garrett could save me from anything. Except from, maybe, I don't know, losing a *Battlestar Galactica* trivia contest. Or from a cyborg. As long as it was on a computer screen, that is.

"And now we wait," he whispered.

"Do we have to wait in the dark?" I whispered back ner-vously. "Can we turn the light back on?"

"No," he said. "I'm sorry, Libby, but we can't. The paranor-mal societies I contacted said most spirits prefer the darkness, and you should make yourself as unobtrusive as possible. Like you're not even there. That way the ghost feels more comfortable with appearing in the environment."

"You contacted paranormal societies?" I was somewhat taken aback. It didn't seem like the kind of thing he'd believe in. But maybe it was part of the whole sci-fi thing.

"Yeah. For research."

"So you're into all that 'the truth is out there' *X-Files* stuff too?" I asked. "You think the ghost is real?"

"I don't." He snorted. "Of course it's not real. It's completely ridiculous. The existence of paranormal phenomena has been repudiated time and time again. And I enjoy science fiction that takes place in an alternate reality, either far into the future or a separate galaxy, so that there's no blurring of reality, like there is in a series such as the *X-Files* or *Supernatural*. The mind can more easily accept the impossible than the implausible—"

"Oh God, spare me," I interrupted. "Let's get it back on track."

"There's no ghost on this ship, Libby," he continued. "That's one of the reasons I wanted to write this story—to figure out what's really going on here. Because even though I know there's no ghost, the eyewitness accounts line up enough to confirm that someone certainly wants us to think so. Now I just have to find out why. But I contacted the paranormal societies, anyway, because a good reporter gets all angles of the story. Even if they don't always line up with his personal convictions."

"Gotcha." I nodded. "Objectivity and all that. Good deal." Even a moment of silence was intolerable. It made me feel like the blackness was pressing in on my eyelids, smothering me.

"But I'm going to tell you right now, it'll be the creepy old lighthouse keeper in a ghost mask. You mark my words."

"Thanks for the tip, Scoobs."

"Oh my God, I am *not* Scooby in this metaphor!" I contested hotly. "Obviously, I'm Daphne!"

"Libby?"

"Yeah?"

"Be quiet."

"Okay."

Silence.

"Garrett, do I have to?"

"Libby, I mean this in the nicest possible way, but shut up."

Slightly longer silence.

"Why?" I whispered so quietly it was barely audible.

"Because I want to be as unobtrusive as possible so that if someone's running around in a ghost suit, he won't know we're here. Or if you want to think about it paranormally, so that the ghost feels comfortable in the environment," he whispered back.

"But what if we *made* the ghost feel comfortable." Brilliant idea! "We could whisper, 'Welcome, spirit,' or something. Or we could sing!" Even more brilliant idea! "Consider yourself at home!" I sang softly. "Consider yourself one of the family."

"Libby," he cut me off.

"Yeah?"

"Even *live* people avoid *Oliver!* My sister was in that, and I wanted to slit my wrists by intermission. Let's steer clear of musical theater, okay?"

"Okay."

Silence.

I sang, "You don't realize how much I need you. Love you all the time and never leave you. Please come on back to me—"

"That's not what I meant," Garrett interrupted again.

"But everybody likes the Beatles."

"Libby," he warned.

"Okay. Quiet. Got it."

We sat, silent, still, in the darkness, as I inched ever closer to Garrett, hoping it would make me feel less scared. It didn't. A lifetime later I had closed my eyes and was almost drifting off to sleep, when I felt a hand cover my mouth.

"Libby," Garrett whispered very, very quietly, "don't move. Don't say anything. Open your eyes very slowly, and don't freak out. Whatever you do, don't scream. I'll take my hand off your mouth if you promise not to scream. Nod if you promise."

I nodded, and he removed his hand as I opened my eyes. My mouth froze in a rictus of horror, hanging open in a silent scream. No sound would have come out even if I'd wanted it to —I was so scared, I couldn't make any noise. There, at the end of the table, was the exact figure I'd heard about. He was much too far away to make out any details, but it was definitely the figure of a man, all in white. I clutched Garrett's right forearm and dug my nails in so fiercely, it was a miracle I didn't draw blood. Luckily, Garrett was a lefty, so he used his free hand to slowly pick up the video camera. Immediately, the ghost retreated into the blackness.

"I'm going to go after it." Garrett got up.

"Don't leave me!" I said, but no sound came out, just air. Garrett vaulted over the cornmeal sacks and chased the figure down the hallway. I immediately flipped the camping lantern on and clung to it like a totem, shaking. Oh God, why was I here? Why didn't I just stay in that awful house? Even Ashling wasn't as bad as a ghost! I mean, yes, maybe she would have killed me eventually, but right now that was a chance I was willing to take.

Moments later Garrett returned.

"You okay?" he asked, bending over to pick up his lantern and flip it on.

I nodded, silent, mouth still frozen in a scream.

"Libby, are you sure?" he asked concernedly. "Here." He shut my jaw for me. "That looks better. Come on, let's go to bed."

"Wh-wha-what about the ghost?" I asked shakily. Words! I'd made words! Progress.

"It disappeared." He kicked a coil of rope with more violence than was necessary. "Whatever it was, a guy in costume or, I don't know, a projection or a hologram or something, it disappeared by the time I got into the hallway."

"Okay."

Garrett led me into the fo'c's'le, closed the door, and bolted it shut. He then helped me up to my bunk. It was like I had lost control of my limbs.

"Libby, are you sure you're okay?" he asked again. "Come on, Proud Mary, you've got this."

"Right." I nodded. "Right, right, I'm fine."

"Sing it with me," he started. "Big wheels keep on turning," he sang tunelessly, totally off-key. "Proud Mary keep on burning."

"Rolling," I sang with him, "rolling. Rolling on the river."

Just like I always told Dev. Sing till you find your happy place. Weird that Garrett knew I did that.

"There you go." Garrett grinned in the glow of his camp light. "That's the Libby Kelting I know."

"Good night, Garrett."

"Good night, Kitty."

I went to bed immediately, but I didn't sleep for a long time.

chapter seven

"And as I slooowly opened my eyes, one millimeter at a time, I saw it appear at the end of the long hallway."

Ten little mouths formed perfectly round *O*'s in a ring around the kitchen table.

"A ghostly figure, all in white," I continued, leaning my elbows into the flour, "and silent as the grave."

"Oooooh," the girls chorused.

"But before we could address the spirit, as mysteriously as it had come, it vanished!" I flourished my rolling pin for emphasis, as they shrieked and clutched each other.

I'd told them this story about five times, but they still clamored for more. And they weren't the only ones who wanted to hear it. I'd become something of a local celebrity since our ghostly sighting.

Practically the moment Garrett's article in the *Camden Crier* hit newsstands, the story was all over Maine and who knew where else. It spread like wildfire. Literally, it was all anyone talked about. I found I enjoyed the ghost a lot more in the daylight—it wasn't scary and I was sort of famous! Even though Garrett's article hadn't mentioned my name to preserve my anonymity, everybody knew I'd been on the boat. Camden Harbor was a small town, and people talked. I was stopped about fifteen times a day on my way in and out of the Bromleigh Homestead and on and off of the *Lettie Mae*.

The best part of all this ghost fuss was that the museum was more crowded than I'd ever seen it. There was even a line outside the fudge shop. A line! There were so many people in the museum they were *waiting* for fudge. The entire staff was running around with huge, dopey grins on their faces. Maddie, who was sporting the standard-issue dopey staff grin, said the museum was reaching attendance levels it hadn't seen since the '70s.

What all this meant, of course, was that we were expecting record numbers for the Fourth of July, which was already traditionally the museum's busiest day. And since yours truly was in charge of the pie table, the pressure was on both in quality and quantity. I mean think about it: pie on the Fourth of July. Ever heard of a little phrase called "American as apple pie"? Yeah. Only like the seminal American dessert on the seminal American holiday. Who wasn't going to want pie? Everyone likes pie.

So after a minor freak-out, I'd decided to use the resources available to me. Upon Miss Libby's Official Decree, this week was "Pie Week" at Girls of Long Ago Camp, and we were cranking out pastry like you would not believe. I'd turned the girls into my personal pie factory. It was a little sweet-shop sweatshop of my very own.

"Guys, don't eat the dough," I said for the millionth time. "It's got lard in it, and that's gross, and I'll get in big trouble if you get salmonella."

"Salmonella?" Emily wrinkled her nose. "There's no fish in this."

"Very funny, miss." She giggled at her own joke.

"Whath thamonella?" Amanda asked.

"Something bad that Lysol kills, as it disinfects to protect, along with ninety-nine percent of other germs," Robin answered her. "Duh. Don't you watch TV?"

"Well, since we're a couple hundred years early for Lysol—as well as TV, for that matter—let's just stay out of the pie crust, okay?"

"Oooookay."

They didn't. Not really. But at least they were eating less of it, minimizing the potential salmonella intake. By the end of cooking time, we'd finished all the lattice-topped and double-crust pies, which meant all we had left to do the rest of the week was crumb-top pies. Not too shabby. This could be the beginning of my very own domestic empire. Martha would be so proud. Except that the whole child-labor aspect might be a problem.

Later that afternoon during craft time, I set up an actual sweatshop in the homestead, as the girls and I sewed flag bunting. Everything everyone did at Camden Harbor that week was in preparation for the Fourth.

"Can you tell uth about the ghotht again, Mith Libby?" Amanda asked, handing me a scrap of fabric into which she'd sewn a truly impressive knot.

"Are you guys sure you want to hear it again?" I attacked the knot. "I've already told it a lot."

The general consensus was yes.

"Okay, then, if you're sure." Man, she'd knotted that up good. "So, Garrett and I were waiting in the galley—"

"This is the point I'm unclear about," Emily interrupted, squinting through her glasses as she threaded a needle. "Who is this Garrett character?"

"He's a reporter at the *Camden Crier.*" I stuck out my tongue, concentrating on undoing the knot.

"And why was he on the boat?"

"He lives there. With me," I answered without thinking about it.

Emily's eyebrow shot up above her glasses.

"Not like that!" Major giggles. "You guys, *not* like that. Stop giggling! It's not like that. He's investigating the ghost, reporting, you know, writing a story. I'm just there to make sure he doesn't steal anything."

"Like your heart?" someone suggested. Giggle, giggle, giggle.

"We are *just friends,*" I said firmly. I mean, um, gross. I couldn't even begin to imagine Garrett as anything other than just a friend. Hobbit feet and Trekkie talk don't exactly inspire romance.

"Suuure," Robin said. "Miss Libby, you know the Jonas Brothers song 'Just Friends'?"

"Can't say that I do." Robin's knowledge of all things Jonas was encyclopedic. Mine, not so much.

"Well," she began with great excitement, as she always did whenever anything Jonas related came up in conversation—which happened a lot more often than you would think in a place where it was technically always supposed to be 1791. "See, Nick Jonas keeps saying that it's cool, 'cause he's just friends with this girl, but everyone knows it's meant to be, and he's making lots of plans, like a picket fence and a rose garden, and thinking about how they're gonna say their vows, which means they get *married.* So even though Nick *said* they were just friends, really he was falling in love, till the end of time. It'll happen," she finished smugly.

"Well, in this case, the Jonas Brothers are mistaken."

Major protests.

"I'm sorry to have to say it — I know it's hard to hear — but just this once the Jonas Brothers are wrong. Garrett and I are friends."

"Men and women can't be friends," Emily said matter-of-factly. "The sex part always gets in the way."

"Seriously." I stared at her. "How old are you?"

"Eight!"

"Hmm." I eyed her suspiciously. I was starting to think she might have been a thirty-five-year-old midget with great skin.

"Miss Libby, you need to resolve your feelings about this Garrett character if you intend to keep pursuing things with Cam. How's that going, by the way?" Emily took a sip of her lemonade. If it had been a cosmo, she would have been ready for *Sex and the City*. Or, more accurately, *Sex and the Harbor*.

The grandfather clock in the parlor tolled two. Saved by the bell. Not that I had any feelings to resolve about Garrett. I knew exactly how I felt about him — he was tolerable. Barely.

"Okay, guys, as educational as this conversation probably is for most of you, we've gotta get you back to the Welcome Center! Darn!"

Emily fixed me with a look that said she knew exactly what I was doing and that I wouldn't be so lucky next time. "How's that going with Cam?" was just not a question I was prepared to answer at the moment. I hadn't seen him since our aborted sail date.

• • •

By the time I'd shepherded all the kids back to their parents, I was more than ready to collapse on the deck of the *Lettie Mae* and read the copy of *His Reluctant Mistress* that I'd liberated from the intern house library, which I was actually enjoying. It wasn't something I was proud of. My newfound appreciation for romance novels was definitely going to stay a secret shame.

Unfortunately, there was a crowd of strangers standing between me and the renowned rake, skilled seducer, and expert spy waiting between the pages of my Harlequin romance. All these unknown people were milling around the boat, blocking my way up the gangplank.

"Um, excuse me," I said as I pushed through the crowd, looking for someone, anyone, I knew. "Excuse me, excuse me."

I spotted Garrett at the front of the crowd.

"Who are all these people?" I asked him under the cover of crowd noise.

"Paranormal societies, mediums, and psychics," he answered.

"Jesus." I scanned the crowd. "Why are they here?"

"To get on the boat. Well, all except Madam Selena." He indicated a woman with wild, curly hair, dressed like a gypsy. "She just wants to feel our energies."

"Our as in yours and mine?"

"Our as in yours and mine," he confirmed.

"I think I'll have a better understanding of the spirit's situation if I can get a better feel for the energies he chose to reveal himself around." Madam Selena poked her headscarf in between us, heavy gold hoops clattering like clunky wind chimes.

"You don't mind, do you?" Garrett whispered. "She's the only one who's been nice. The rest of them are really pushy."

"No, that's fine," I agreed. "Please, Madam Selena," I said at a normal volume. "I'd love it if you, um, read my energy."

"Ah, blessed be." She smiled beatifically. Madam Selena closed her eyes, inhaled deeply, and held up her hennaed hand in front of my face, about three inches from my nose. Two minutes of silence later, she smiled and opened her eyes.

"What a lovely, romantic, watery glow coming off of this one." She waved her hand around my head, bangles clattering up and down her arm.

"Watery?" I asked.

"Yes, yes. You must be a water sign. Am I right?" I nodded. She was pretty good. "I'm feeling . . . Pisces. Pisces?" Again, I nodded. Actually, she was really good.

"And you." She turned to Garrett and repeated the process. Only this time, her smile was even wider. "Scorpio," she said definitively. "Determined Scorpio. The natural investigators of the zodiac!"

"Actually, yeah." Garrett looked stunned. No surprise, given his complete dismissal of everything supernatural and paranormal. "I am. That's amazing. I can't believe it. How did you—"

"Hey, Libs." Cam worked his way into the circle and kissed me on the cheek, like he'd never been gone. Like he hadn't avoided me all week. Like we'd just seen each other. "You look . . . busy," he said, eyeing Madam Selena skeptically, and she returned the look.

"Are you a fire sign, young man?" Madam Selena asked him imperiously.

"I'm not a sign of anything. What the fuck is she talking about?" he muttered into my ear, just loud enough for Madam Selena to overhear.

"On what day were you born?" she said with a sigh.

"April fifth," he answered suspiciously. "Why?"

"Aries." She nodded. "The ram."

"Yeah." Cam looked Madam Selena up and down, like she was a total loon and he couldn't be bothered to deal with her. "I've gotta go. I'll see you later, Libs." He swaggered off, presumably to his own boat. Madam Selena watched him go, a worried look on her face.

"My lovely, romantic Pisces," Madam Selena said, beckoning me away from the circle. I followed her as she crooked a finger at me.

"Yes?"

"Be careful, little fish." She grabbed my wrist. "Fiery Aries is quick to temper, and their selfish, hot-blooded passions often lead them to promiscuity. More so than any other sign. The ram has not the fierce loyalty and emotional depth that draws the fish to its natural mate, the scorpion, whose union is blessed by lifelong passion as a true joining of souls. Guard your heart." She leaned down and kissed my forehead. "Blessed be."

"Um, you too."

Madam Selena's jewelry tinkled as she walked off into the ether. Fish and scorpions? It was hard to take any advice seriously when it concerned various disparate members of the animal kingdom. But even though she was a little strange, she was nice, and she smelled like patchouli. I liked her. I made my way back into the circle and stood at Garrett's side.

"Okay, now who are the rest of these people?" I asked.

"BAGS, ma'am," a guy with a close-shaved beard and a

baseball hat answered for Garrett, shaking my hand vigorously.

"Bags? Like under your eyes?" I patted my under-eye area for emphasis. "Or like shopping!"

"No, actually, neither." Garrett swallowed something that sounded suspiciously like a chuckle. "BAGS. The Bureau of Accredited Ghost Slayers."

"We're not all BAGS!" a housewife-looking woman contradicted shrilly, joining Beardy at the front. "Paranormal Enthusiasts of Maine. Pleased to meet you."

"BAGS," Beardy began, "is the nation's premier paranormal investigative society. We promise to bring professionalism, personality, and confidentiality to each case we investigate. You ever heard of *Ghost Slayers*?"

"What, like on the Syfy channel?" I asked, not that I'd ever watched the Syfy channel, but their ads were all over every magazine I'd ever read. They were impossible to miss.

"Exactly." Beardy grinned.

Housewife, looking worried, jumped in. "We are not a cheap thrill-seeking publicity stunt of a television show," she sniffed. "We are not affiliated with any forms of media. Our society is an experienced group of professionals dedicated to the study and research of paranormal activity, using the latest in technology and scientific techniques to claim or disclaim the possible existence of paranormal phenomenon, not to raise Nielsen ratings."

"*We* are not amateurs," countered BAGS, as if to emphasize that the Mainers were. "We're one of the only nationally recognized paranormal societies, not a group of bored housewives and off-duty bus drivers." Housewife's nostrils flared. "We've had extensive experience. The BAGS plan brings a levelheaded and comfortable atmosphere into your home, or, uh, ship, to listen to your experiences and concerns, to help you understand the nature of the problem by supplying you with the information you need to understand why this is happening. We then set up equipment and begin trying to recreate and debunk personal experiences in an attempt to find good evidence either for or against paranormal activity."

"There is no 'plan' at the Paranormal Enthusiasts of Maine," Housewife said smugly. "We use professional clairvoyants and mediums to custom-tailor our investigation to your specific spirit's needs."

"Come on, man." Beardy tried out a new tactic: approaching Garrett from a "bro" angle. "We like to have fun. We are, after all, *normal people*." He made a crazy sign at Housewife. "Heck, I don't think any of us even watch *Star Trek*. Heh, heh, heh."

Ooh, bad move. Beardy had just insulted sci-fi in front of Garrett. He had no idea what he was in for. Garrett took a deep breath, about to go into lecture mode.

"Okay." I headed him off at the pass before he could get going. "What is it you guys want?"

"To get on the boat!" Beardy and Housewife answered simultaneously.

"Like I said, I'm not authorized to do that." Garrett shrugged. "You'll have to come back tomorrow and take it up with museum personnel. I'm more than happy to answer your questions, but I can't let you on the ship."

"Dude, be cool," Beardy tried again.

"Sorry, no," Garrett said firmly. "Press conference over." He placed his hand squarely on my back and steered me up to the deck of the *Lettie Mae*, securing the rope over the entrance to the ship that meant the *Lettie* was closed for the night. I peered apprehensively over the side, half afraid a mob of aggressive ghost hunters was going to rush the gangplank and storm the ship. The paranormal enthusiasts muttered discontentedly and milled about, but made no move to enter the ship by force.

"Sit-in at the president's office!" Housewife yelled suddenly. "Protest! Let's park ourselves outside his office! And we're not moving until we get on that boat!"

The half of the crowd from Maine roared its approval.

"What do we want?" she shouted. "Onto the boat! When do we want it? NOW!"

The rest of the Paranormal Enthusiasts of Maine took up the chant and followed their leader to the president's office. After deliberating for a moment, Beardy gathered his camera crew and left, hot on their trail, the boom-mike man bringing up the rear.

"Yikes," I said as we watched them go off, "this is not good. President Harrow isn't going to be happy about this. The museum is not going to like this one bit. Not one little bit."

"No?" Garrett watched them too.

"No." I shook my head. "Well, Roger will be thrilled," I corrected myself. "The Syfy channel? He'll be over the moon. But the rest of them . . ." I trailed off ominously.

"What's so bad about it?"

"Most of the staff were apprehensive at best about the whole ghost thing, if not openly hostile. This is exactly what they feared: turning the museum into some kind of media circus or exploiting the ghost as a publicity stunt. They want to avoid anything that has any potential to damage the museum's credibility. And I know the office is *technically* off the museum grounds, but people will still complain that a camp of clairvoyants and camera crews will shatter the illusion."

"What illusion?" He adjusted his glasses.

"The illusion that in here, it's always 1791, obviously."

"Libby, I hate to break it to you, but they sell Bud Light and chicken fingers in the Golden Plough Tavern. The illusion's been shattered."

"You know what I mean." I swatted his arm playfully. "But seriously, Garrett, this could be bad. I'm worried."

"About what?"

"Well, what if they decide that this whole thing has gotten out of control and shut it down?"

"Shut it down? What do you mean?"

"I mean they might kick out all the media and release an official statement denying any knowledge or evidence of paranormal activity."

"You don't want them to kick out the media?" The corners of his mouth twitched. "You'd miss that guy from *Ghost Slayers,* wouldn't you? I could see you checking him out."

"No, you idiot, you!" I yelled in exasperation. "I don't want them to kick you out!"

"You don't? You mean you'd be upset if I left? If we couldn't live on the boat together?" he asked carefully.

"Well, of course! I don't want to go back to living with Ashling. If they kick you out, I'm off the boat too. And I can't go back to Ashling. I just can't."

Garrett's smile faded. "Oh, right. Yeah. Ashling. Of course," he said gruffly.

"Yeah. Obviously." I shot him a funny look, but he didn't notice. An oddly loaded silence hung between us.

"You're going to the Fourth of July Lobsterfest fireworks thing, right?" I eventually asked, to break the silence.

"Of course," he said stoically. "Everyone in Camden Harbor goes. I've gone every year since I was born. I don't see why this year should be any different."

"Oh, that's right," I mused. "I always forget that you grew up here. And Cam did too, right?" Shoot. I hadn't meant to mention the C-word, because Garrett seemed to tweak out whenever it came up. But it just popped out.

"Technically, Cam grew up in the greater Rockport area," Garrett said, clenching his jaw, which I was beginning to recognize as the sign of a seriously pissed-off Garrett, "but basically, yes. All the towns in the county feed into the same regional high school. He was in my sister's class."

"The one who was in *Oliver!*?"

"Uh, yeah." He seemed surprised that I remembered. "She just graduated from Tulane. And to the delight of theatergoers everywhere, she is *not* pursuing a career on the American musical stage."

I laughed, which seemed to jolt him slightly out of his ill humor.

"Sun's setting." I nodded in a westerly direction. No red sky tonight, just the sun dipping straight down into the water.

"I guess I'd better get ghost hunting." He sighed.

"I wouldn't mind bringing Madam Selena with us, would you?" I asked. "I like her. And maybe her patchouli would clean out some of the fishy smell in the galley."

"Maybe." He laughed. "I don't know how we could bring her in and leave out the other ones, though."

"True." I mulled it over. "I really don't want seventy-five ghost hunters in here."

"Regardless, tonight it's just me." He pushed off the rail he'd been leaning against and straightened. "Down into the hold."

"Can I come with you again?" I asked tentatively. "This time I'll be quieter, I promise. Well, I promise to try," I said truthfully.

"Really? You want to come again?" We went belowdecks.

"Garrett, I'm gonna be honest." I sighed. "It's really creepy being all alone in the fo'c's'le. And yes, it's creepy in the dark galley too, but you're there, you know? So it's not so bad."

"Yeah." He pulled out our camping lanterns. "I'll be there."

Garrett switched on the light, illuminating the darkness. We shone.

chapter eight

Was there no end to the humiliation Roger the publicist would force me to endure? I was starting to think the man had a personal vendetta against me. To man the pie table, he'd dressed me as Betsy Ross. And I don't mean as a nice, historically accurate Philadelphia upholsterer. No, I had on a giant mobcap and a white-starred blue dress with layers of red and white ruffled sleeves and a red and white striped overskirt with huge panniers. It looked like America had thrown up on me. When Ashling spotted me, she almost choked on her own bile, eyes bugging out of her head, before she ran off, presumably to tell off someone in charge. This time I could hardly blame her. Seriously, this was a travesty, particularly for any aspiring historian with a modicum of self-respect.

I tucked an escaping curl back under my mobcap. How was it the Fourth of July already? It felt like summer was speeding by.

A customer claimed my attention, jolting me out of my daydreaming. As I'd predicted, the pie table had been quite popular, second only to my next-door neighbor, the lemonade barrel, which Suze had somehow been coerced into running. I cut a slice of blueberry lattice top and handed it over on a not-so-historical patriotic paper plate.

"Hey, Suze, can I have some lemonade? It's really hot today." I fanned myself with a ruffle, but it didn't help. I was just stuffed into too many layers.

"Of course." She handed me a patriotic paper cup. "It *is* hot." She wiped some sweat away from under the brim of a small, jaunty tricorn hat festooned with red, white, and blue cockades.

Roger had dressed Suze as Molly Pitcher—get it? Lemonade? Pitcher? The wit of Roger never ceased to amaze me— the semi-folkloric woman who'd given water to Washington's troops and manned her husband's cannon in the Revolutionary War. Her outfit was a lot less unfortunate than mine. It involved a long blue skirt and a red and blue militia jacket tailored for a woman. It was pretty cute, actually. But Roger had forced her tote around one of those long sticks used to stuff cannons, so it was pretty much a lose-lose situation.

The various vendors—us, beer, ice cream, candy, souvenirs —were ringed in a circle around the town green, leaving the middle open for everyone to mill around. The lobsters, roasted corn, and clambake were under a giant tent filled with long picnic tables on the beach. I think Ashling was pounding crabs with a hammer down there, but I hadn't asked Suze for specifics. We chatted as the afternoon passed, dispensing pie and lemonade to a large, spirited crowd of holiday revelers.

"Excuse me," said a thin, balding, redheaded man with wire-framed glasses after he took a contemplative bite of apple pie. "Is that a hint of cardamom I detect in the crumb topping?"

"Why yes—yes, it is," I stammered, taken aback.

"Unusual. It's an inspired choice." He continued chewing.

"And I'm going to say . . . cinnamon, nutmeg, cloves, and ginger—fresh grated ginger—in the filling."

"Yes." Oh my God. Red hair. Glasses. Way too informed about spices. Could it be?

"A lard-based crust, now there's something you don't see every day." He smiled fondly at his forkful of pie. "But it produces a uniquely flaky crust and tender crumb. It might be time for lard to make a comeback."

Dev, if he was still alive, would not be pleased.

The man finished his pie and put the empty plate down. "I'm Frank Sinskey," he introduced himself.

"Emily's dad?" I shook his hand.

"Yes." He chuckled. "Slight family resemblance, huh? And you must be Miss Libby." I nodded. "Did you make this pie?" Again nod. "It's good. Really good."

Frank Sinskey rubbed his jaw, thinking, which was lucky for me, because I'd gone slack jawed and had lost the ability to produce coherent thought, so I couldn't have answered a question if he'd asked one.

"I think I'd like to do a piece on classic—really classic—American desserts. I'll pitch it to the magazine after the holiday weekend." He handed me a business card—the words *Bon Appétit* glittered in the sun. "Call me when you have a minute to talk."

Oh my God. Oh my *GOD!!* He liked my pie! *Bon*-freaking-*Appétit* liked my pie! I waved mutely as he walked off, mouth hanging open in a dopey grin. This was a Fourth of July miracle! I mean, yes, there was a chance that this was part of an enormous Mono Corps conspiracy, and they were just using another of their magazines in an evil plot to eradicate everything Dev held near and dear. But more likely, the man just liked my pie.

"Hey, sweetie pie." It was Cam, leaning against the table. I hadn't even noticed him approach, enveloped as I was in a hazy *Bon Appétit*–induced glow. "Get it? Sweetie pie?" I nodded, grinning dumbly. "You got any sweetie pies for your sweetie pie? On the house?" he asked sweetly.

Not even conscious of moving my arms, I somehow cut a slice of blueberry crumb top.

"You okay? You seem weird." He eyed me askance, taking a giant bite.

"*Bon Appétit* likes my pie," I said dazedly.

"Uh, okay." I don't think he had any idea what I was talking about. "Listen, when do you get off?"

"After the sun goes down. Just in time for the fireworks."

"Right." He started looking around the green. "I'd love to stay and keep you company here, babe, but I can't." He pulled a frown. "So I'll come watch the fireworks with you, okay?"

"Okay."

"Yo, Scrubs!" he shouted suddenly at someone across the green. "This shit is good! Come have some pie! What? Yeah, yeah! Beer me!" He kissed my cheek. "Later, Libs." He went off to join the mysterious Scrubs, whom I'd still never seen, making his way through the crowds across the green.

"Libby, that's unbelievable," Suze said quietly.

"I know, right? I don't think Scrubs is a real name either. It all seems a little fishy to me." I looked around the green, searching for this "Scrubs" character.

"No, Libby, I meant *Bon Appétit.*" She shook her head. "That's incredible. You should be really proud." She smiled. "Now I've really got to try a piece of that pie. Cut it."

We split a piece of apple, watching as the crowd gathered around a small clearing dead center in the town green.

"Here ye, here ye!" President Harrow bellowed over the microphone. "Welcome, one and all, to the celebration of the birth of our great nation! Hip, hip, huzzah!" The crowd *huzzah*ed right along with him. Appropriately enough, President Harrow was dressed as our nation's father, the first president, George Washington. His white periwig was too big for his wrinkled head and kept sliding around, and he was trying to talk through what looked like an actual set of fake wooden teeth. Ah, what a great day to be an American.

"I'm very happy to welcome you all here today, and right now I'm especially happy to be out of my office!" The crowd laughed, well aware that the Paranormal Enthusiasts of Maine were still camped out outside the president's office. Beardy and the Ghost Slayers, however, had decided to join in the fun. At the moment they were nibbling corn on the cob and drinking beer. The sound guy had traded out his boom mike for a giant red balloon.

"Before we kick things off with a bang" — the president gestured to the Revolutionary militia now standing in formation in the middle of the green — "I have a few brief announcements. First, fireworks begin at sundown! Don't miss 'em! Second, if you wish to order the full New England Clambake Dinner, please place your orders now. And finally, the End-of-Season Costume Ball will be upon us before we know it, so I hope you've all started working on your getups!"

"Getups?" I repeated.

"The focus of the Costume Ball is on period clothing," Suze said. "I mean yes, of course, there's music and dancing, but a lot of it is more like a fashion show or costume contest. Any style from the latter half of the eighteenth century is permissible. I think there's a costume rental shop in Rockport, but most of the hard-core historians sew their own clothing using period patterns and techniques."

"They make their own clothes? Seventeen hundreds style? That's insane," I whispered. "People actually do that?"

"Ashling's already started hers."

"Of course she has."

"She's using a whalebone needle and everything." Suze raised her eyebrows.

Well, I was no Ashling. There was no way I could have sewn a ball gown by hand. Frankly, I wasn't totally sure I could sew a ball gown even with a sewing machine, my sewing strengths being more of the decorative-craft variety, so at least I had the renting option to fall back on. Because nothing was going to keep me from that ball.

President Harrow tapped on the microphone for attention. "And now that we've dealt with that ball, let's have fun with some more balls!"

A pack of Squaddies hanging out by the beer vendor roared with laughter. I was too far away to see, but I could've sworn President Harrow winked.

"Musket balls! Cannonballs! Not that any balls will actually be fired, of course," he assured us. "Just loud noises and puffs of smoke! No deaths by accidental shooting this year!" Suze and I exchanged glances. "Men of the Seventy-second Maine Light

Infantry, our very own Revolutionary reenactment militia, take it away!"

Boom! Shots rang out across the field, covering us all in a haze of smoke, as a fife and drum corps started up. Playing a spirited "Yankee Doodle Dandy," the fife and drums appeared at the edge of the town green and marched in a ring around it. Suze and I clapped our hands in time to the music. Between this and the sea shanties, colonial Americans must have been really peppy. This stuff made Britney Spears sound downright glum.

"Yes, my romantic little Pisces! Dream to the music! Release your creative subconscious! See with the third eye!" Madam Selena had drifted over to our table, grooving along to the fifes.

"Hi, Madam Selena." I smiled. "Happy Fourth of July!"

"Oh, I don't celebrate the holiday," she said airily. "I was merely drawn to the profusion of positive energies congregating here." She drew a circle in the air with one turquoise-ringed finger. "I haven't seen such a large golden aura in years."

Suze looked confused.

"Would you like a piece of pie, Madam Selena?" I asked. "It's on the house."

"Why, yes, thank you." She inclined her head. "May I read your tarot in exchange? As a barter? A brief reading only."

"Why . . . um . . . sure. Yeah, I guess so."

"Blueberry lattice, please," she requested as she withdrew a battered deck of cards from the folds of her skirt. She shuffled them on the counter as I sliced her a piece of pie. She fanned them out before me. "Choose three, one at a time, then place them face-up on the counter."

I picked the first. "Past," she said as the card hit the table. "Present," the next, and finally, "Future." She leaned in to examine them.

"Hmm . . ." She stroked the cards. "Past: Queen of Swords Reversed. A deceitful, sly, intolerant, and narrow-minded woman, expert in the use of half-truths and quiet slander."

"Ashling," Suze whispered, stunned. "Wow, she's good."

"I know, right?" I whispered back.

Looking troubled, Madam Selena stroked the second card. "Present: Temperance Reversed. Imbalance. Volatility. Poor judgment. Fickle decisions. Conflicting interests." She shook her head worriedly. "Two reverse cards. Careful, little fish."

Suze looked equally worried, scowling somewhat owlishly behind her glasses.

"Ah, but the future." Madam Selena breathed a sigh of relief as she caressed the third card, smiling beautifully. "The Lovers." I blushed. "Ah, love is a force that makes you choose and decide for reasons you often can't understand. Finding something or someone who is so much a part of yourself that you cannot, dare not resist. There are choices to be made, but in the end, harmony and union."

Suze made an *ooh* face.

"Persevere, little fish, happiness will be yours." Madam Selena collected her cards and returned them to her garments. "*Ad astris per aspera*— to the stars through difficulties." She picked up her pie. "Blessed be." She wandered away aimlessly.

"Blessed be," I called after her.

"Love is a force that makes you choose and decide." Suze mulled it over. "That's actually quite profound."

"Yeah. It does sound profound," I agreed. "Madam Selena's very good."

"I know! Ashling! The cards knew!" Suze squeaked. "Then I guess you'd better be careful with all that temperance reversed business. I'd stay away from the beer."

"That's not a problem."

We discussed the tarot at length until all the pies were gone and Suze was scraping the bottom of the lemonade barrel. The timing worked out almost perfectly, the sun setting as I sold my last piece of pie. As twilight fell, I stacked the empty pie tins, broke down the collapsible table, and neatly folded the flag bunting that had decorated it.

"Okay." Suze huffed and puffed. "I've got to roll this barrel back to the cooper's shop."

"Are you serious?" I asked, concerned. "That thing's enormous!" It was. It was almost as tall as Suze and way more than twice as round.

"Oh, not to worry!" She struggled. "I'll just pop it up there and be back in a jiff! Go turn in your pie tins."

"Suze, are you sure? I really don't mind helping you —"

"Nope, nope, I got it." She set her glasses determinedly. "I can do this myself."

"Well . . . okay . . . if you're sure . . ."

Red faced, Suze rolled away her barrel, moving at a glacial pace. I shrugged and collected my pie tins. I brought them back to the Bromleigh Homestead, to be washed on Monday. Probably leaving them in a bucket outside overnight wasn't the best idea, as every raccoon in the county would come running, but I wanted to find Cam before the fireworks started, so we could watch them together. After the tins clattered into the bucket, I wiped my hands on my skirt and headed to the green to look for Cam.

They were going to be shooting the fireworks off a boat anchored offshore in the harbor. Nearly every square inch of the green was covered in picnic blankets, with families settling in to watch. I picked my way carefully around the blankets, scanning the unfamiliar faces for Cam, but he was nowhere to be found. It got darker and darker, and I began to despair of ever finding him. Maybe he was on the beach — even though the main Fourth of July festivities were taking place on the green, you'd probably have a good view of the fireworks from the beach. I hitched up my skirts and ran toward the shore.

I heard a crackle and a hiss, and looked up to the sky — oh no! The first opening volleys of the fireworks display. Where could he be? I hit the beach and scrambled up the stone jetty, hoping to get a better view. Peering into the dark, the beach appeared to be completely deserted. The wind whipped my skirts and teased my hair out from under my mobcap. Oh, where, where could he be?

"Libby! Hey, Libby! Is that you?"

Another slight hiss and crackle, as a small shower of starbursts rained down. I turned — Garrett was climbing up the other side of the jetty.

"Oh, hey, Garrett." I ran carefully over the uneven stones to meet him, as the waves crashed on the side of the jetty. "Listen, have you seen —"

BOOM! An enormous firework exploded, filling the sky

with white-gold lights and making the beach bright as day. In the moment that we were illuminated, suddenly and without warning, Garrett leaned down and kissed me.

Like really kissed me. Like movie-kissed me. No, like *epic* movie–kissed me. This was a *Titanic, Doctor Zhivago, Gone with the Wind* kiss. The fireworks exploded around us, a booming, symphonic underscore, turning the world green and blue and gold as we were bathed in falling sparks.

I had no idea how long we were on that jetty. Time had stopped. Except it clearly hadn't, because eventually there was silence. Startled by the quiet, I broke the kiss. In the distance the applause from the town green floated toward us.

"Oh my God." I pulled away, white faced. What had I done? How had this even happened? Garrett didn't even like me. And I sure as hell didn't like him.

"Libby, I know that was sudden, but I have to tell you. I—"

"No, Garrett. Don't," I cut him off.

"Libby, please," he pleaded. "You have to know how I feel. I—"

"Don't. Don't say it. Don't say anything."

"But—but why?" He looked hurt and confused. "I don't understand. I—"

"I'm—I'm here with Cam," I stuttered.

"Really? Really, Libby? You're here with Cam?" Garrett said angrily. "Then where the hell is he? He's sure as hell not here." Garrett ran a hand through his hair, fighting the wind as it disarrayed his locks. "Libby, I'm here. I'm here with you."

"I should go find him."

"Jesus, Libby." He shook his head. "You're so much better than this," he said sadly.

"Better than this? Than him? Are you kidding?" I said.

"Libby, you—"

"Better?" I kept talking right over Garrett, not even really hearing what he'd said. "Better? There is no one better, Garrett. Cam's practically perfect. He's like one of the nicest guys I've ever met. So sweet. And romantic. And . . . chivalrous."

Garrett snorted.

"He's a gentleman, Garrett. A real one. You know, you could learn a thing or two from Cam."

"You deserve so much better, Libby. You—"

"Deserve what, Garrett? What? You think I deserve . . . you?" I asked somewhat hysterically. "Because you're so much better than he is? Is that what you're saying? That you think you're better than he is? You've got to be kidding." An ugly laugh burbled up before I could stop it. It echoed, hanging between us in the night.

Garrett recoiled like I'd slapped him.

"You know what? Save it, Libby." He turned away to look out over the water. "I don't need to hear any more."

"Look." I exhaled noisily. I had to make peace. There was no other choice. "We have to live on a boat together for the rest of the summer." He laughed mirthlessly. "Why don't we just chalk this up to, um, holiday spirits and just pretend none of it ever happened, okay? Just go back to being friends."

"Friends. Sure, Libby. If that's what you want," he said bitterly. "Friends."

"I . . . I do." I tentatively reached for his hand, willing to make peace—at least for the sake of domestic harmony. He shook me off.

"Go find your boyfriend, Libby." He turned away, sticking

his hands in his pockets, watching the waves break over the end of the jetty.

"Okay," I said in a small voice. "I'll see you back on the boat, then."

He didn't respond. I climbed down the jetty and watched him as I ran, a hunched figure standing alone on the rocks, buffeted on both sides by waves breaking low in the water.

I ran away from the beach and back toward the green. Oh God, I was a horrible person. How could I have done something like that to Cam? To sweet, romantic, perfectly perfect Cam? And with Garrett of all people? Garrett! I was a horrible, horrible person. A horrible, *confused* person. I mean, Cam and I were dating. Sort of. Not that we'd ever talked about it, really . . . but I definitely shouldn't be running around kissing other people. Right? I mean, especially kissing *friends* . . . whom I *lived with* . . . whom I didn't even like . . . I mean, it was Garrett! Obnoxious, arrogant, self-important, completely lame, totally nerdy, terribly dressed Garrett! How had this even happened? But oh, that kiss . . .

BLEEEEAAAGGGGGGGGGH.

The unmistakable sound of vomit hitting ground interrupted my tumultuous thoughts. I peered into the bush I'd just passed.

"Cam?"

Sure enough, Cam was crouched on all fours, heaving into a bush. Temperance reversed, indeed.

"Hey, Libs." He smiled crookedly, wiping his mouth. "I couldn't find you." He hurled again. "I don't feel so good."

"Yeah, I can see that." I knelt down to join him. "Come on, let's get up. I'll help you."

"Aw, you're too good for me, Libs," he said, becoming increasingly maudlin and tearing up a bit. "You're like an angel. You're my angel. Save me, little red, white, and blue angel."

"Yeah, yeah, I've got you, Cam." I helped him up. "You're okay. I've got you. Where should we go?"

"Travis." He spat a neat stream of puke into the bushes. "He's my ride."

"Pirate Travis?" Cam nodded. "Then, let's go find him."

He was easy to spot. The Dread Pirate Travis was now dressed like Uncle Sam, handing out sparklers in the middle of the town green. I lumbered over to Uncle Sam, Cam leaning heavily on my shoulder.

"Hey." Travis nodded sympathetically, in a sign of solidarity at our ridiculous outfits. "Dude, I think this museum is just out to get us." He stroked his fake white beard, which was slipping off his chin to the left.

"I'm starting to think you're right, Travis."

"But this time I get to tell kids to play with fire, so that's cool." He cheerfully handed a sparkler to a small boy with brown hair.

"Yeah . . . um, listen, Travis." I tried to readjust Cam so he was less heavy, but to no avail. He was crushing my shoulder. "I think Cam had too much to drink—"

"Dude, he and Scrubs invented the most hilarious drinking game! So, you take four beers, a sparkler, and—"

"Tell me about it later," I interrupted. "Listen, he's really sick, and he told me you were his ride home?"

"Yeah." Uncle Sam pulled on his beard. "I have to finish out my shift here, and then I'll take him home and get him some water and stuff. Just sit him down and lean him up against that cannon. I'll make sure he doesn't pass out and choke on his own vomit."

"Thanks. That's . . . sweet."

"No biggie, Betsy Ross." Struggling, I eased Cam into a semi-comfortable position next to the cannon. His head lolled, and he grinned blankly.

"You're my angel, Libs." Cam heaved and vomited heavily onto the hem of my Betsy Ross dress. Now America really had thrown up on me. "You're the nicest person I know." He retched a little, but nothing came up. Then he passed out.

"Don't worry, I got it." Uncle Sam handed me a sparkler. "Happy Fourth of July, Betsy Ross."

I took it and walked off into the night. The nicest person? Hardly. I was the type of person who betrayed a boy who'd never been anything but nice to me, who had finally shown me that romance and chivalry weren't dead, by kissing some obnoxious loser. The type of person who probably deserved to be covered in vomit. Ugh! Gross! This was even worse than pork fat! Too many thoughts were careening around in my already stuffed brain, and I just wanted them to be quiet. I started running. Running away—from Cam, from Garrett, from everything. For the first time since I'd arrived in Camden Harbor, I wished I was up at Moose Lake with Mom, Dad, and the beagles, where I'd spent every summer before this, and where everything was so much less . . . complicated. Using the sparkler to light my way, I ran until I somehow ended up outside the boathouse, with a stitch in my side from trying to do cardio in a corset. I leaned against the weather-beaten wooden planks and sunk to my knees, curling into a ball against the boathouse wall. The sparkler went out, plunging me into darkness. As I listened to the waves crash against the dock, soundless tears poured down my cheeks. I buried my face in my hands, trying to drown out my thoughts with the roar of the ocean.

chapter nine

True to his word, Garrett pretended that nothing had happened. Neither one of us was doing a particularly good job of pretending, however. All of the next week, we were painfully conscious of each other as we tried to navigate the minuscule shared space of the fo'c's'le without making physical contact, which was practically impossible.

Garrett was being so carefully, formally polite that I half expected him to ask me if I would be attending the assemblies at Bath, and did I not find society in the country dreadfully dull after a season in town? Maybe that was why he'd borrowed my copy of *Northanger Abbey*—to pick up tips. That was the longest conversation we'd had all week:

"Can I borrow your book?"

"Um . . . this one?" I held up *Northanger Abbey*. I assumed he hadn't meant *Let Sleeping Rogues Lie* or *Never Seduce a Scoundrel*.

"Yes."

"Uh, sure."

So we were surviving, but it wasn't exactly pleasant. I was considering asking Madam Selena to move in just to break the tension. Or exorcise some of these negative energies.

Beardy would have definitely moved in. It was hard to believe, but the Paranormal Enthusiasts of Maine were *still* camped out at President Harrow's. And it had been weeks. Weeks! Beardy, however, had decided to stalk me and Garrett. He spent most of his time loitering around outside the boat, waving to us whenever one of our heads happened to peek over the side. It was a little creepy. I had a newfound sympathy for Britney Spears.

So between the paranormal paparazzi and the elephant in the fo'c's'le, I was spending as much time as humanly possible out of the ship. As per usual, Girls of Long Ago Camp was proving to be my salvation. I'd thrown myself wholeheartedly into an ambitious quilting project. Perhaps overly ambitious, but I was trying to fill all the corners of my brain with binding and batting, so that there would be no room for nerdy reporters who were disturbingly good kissers . . .

"Mith Libby?" I snapped out of it. Amanda was standing in front of the parlor window that faced the street, looking worried. "Thomething jutht hit the window."

"Okay, don't worry." I stood up, moving my quilt blocks to the floor. "Let's see what it is." I joined her at the window.

"I think it wath that." She pointed at a small rock by the gardenia bush under the windowsill that had what looked like a piece of parchment tied to it with a silk ribbon.

"I'll go get it." Now I was curious too. "Guys, I'll be right back, okay? Please don't stab each other with the needles!" I called as I went out the front door. They giggled.

I knelt on the front step and leaned into the gardenia bush to pick up the rock. Yep, that was definitely a piece of parchment. Rock in hand, I went back into the house. Not that I actually thought a quilt fight would break out, but better safe than sorry.

"What wath it?" Amanda asked as she joined me in the entryway.

I untied the ribbon. There was a note written on the parchment in ink. I read:

> "You left something on our steps.
>   SF"

SF? SF?! I didn't know anyone named . . . ohhh right. Susannah Fennyweather. Ashling. So I'd left something on the steps back at the house? Impossible. Unless, of course, my belongings had somehow started moving around on their own. Everything I owned in Camden Harbor was either on the boat or stored in that rickety IKEA closet. How weird.

Amanda was still waiting expectantly.

"Oh, it's nothing," I explained. "Apparently I left something in the house I used to live at."

"Why didn't they just text you?" Robin asked from the couch.

"Because that would be way too normal," I answered.

I cleaned up, got the girls to the Welcome Center, and changed back into my giant blue polo as quickly as possible, curiosity eating me alive. What the hell could be on those steps? I sprinted down the sidewalk to the house. It looked exactly the same as it always did, except with one unusual addition.

A short, skeletally thin Indian boy with spiked hair was sitting on the steps next to a Louis Vuitton hat box and a Bernina sewing machine, licking an enormous swirl of soft-serve ice cream with rainbow sprinkles.

"Dev! Oh my God, Dev! What happened?! Are you okay?!" I sprinted up the steps. "Jesus Christ, you're like malnourished."

"I know, right?" He licked his cone. "I'm like an effing UNI-CEF ad. Save the Children!"

"Did they not feed you in New York?"

"Emaciated is the new black, darling. But not for me. Not anymore. I'm on an all–ice cream diet until people stop asking if they can sponsor me for a dime a day."

"Well, you picked the right place. You've got the Sea Swirl for soft-serve, and then the Dairy Bar is the best homemade ice cream in the world. Try the S'mores!"

"Yes, that's why I picked Camden Harbor as my safe house. For the ice cream," he said sarcastically. "Why aren't you wearing pants?"

"I'm wearing pants!" I shouted.

"Show me," he demanded. I flashed some khaki.

"Why are you here, Dev?" I joined him on the step. "What happened?"

"I got fired," he said matter-of-factly. "I put full-fat milk in someone's latte."

"Yikes."

"And I was afraid they were going to kill me. Full-fat milk? I mean, really! Maybe I deserved to die. But I was just so tired, I wasn't paying attention. So the minute they fired me, I got on a Greyhound bus bound for points north. To go to the only place I could think of where Mono Corps could never find me. And to see you, of course." He bit off a piece of waffle cone.

"Well, you picked a good place to hide from the fashionistas. People wear *Tevas* here."

"No!" He gasped. "Libby, how have you *survived?!*"

"I'm tougher than I look," I said. "How did you find this place?"

"Oh, I asked for directions to the intern house at the Welcome Center. I told them I was visiting a friend. But then I knocked on the door, and this girl in a *whale* T-shirt, worn unironically, might I add"—he made a face—"told me you didn't live here anymore, and she, quote, 'would not be a party to Libby's man parade.'" He smirked. "And I couldn't come in." He paused to take another bite of ice cream. "If, unlikely though it may be, you *are* having a man parade, however, I would like to be a party to that party," he added.

"Well, she's right—I don't live there anymore. She should've let you in, though. It wasn't very nice to make you wait on the step. Not that I'm surprised," I huffed.

"Well, where do you live?"

"In a tiny room. On a boat." He raised an eyebrow. "With a boy." Double-eyebrow raise. "Not like that!"

"What's it like?" he asked suspiciously.

"Purely professional. We live together in a business-only, investigative capacity."

"I have no idea what that means." He licked his ice cream nonchalantly. "And I have no idea where I'm going to stay."

"Well, you can stay with me. On the boat."

"I thought you said it was like really tiny."

"Yeah, it is. But so are you. We'll put you somewhere." I could build him some kind of nest out of blankets, and he could curl up in a ball in the two square feet of space in the fo'c's'le. Or something.

"You sure I'm not breaking up your love nest?"

"I am totally, completely sure," I reassured him. He was breaking up my awkward nest, but that was so not a problem. "I should warn you, though—it's haunted."

"Um, oooookay." He rolled his eyes. "Sure, Libby. Whatever you say."

"Would someone PLEASE get the *trash* off the step!" Ashling yelled from inside the house.

"Come on." I stood up. "Let's go. I can take you to the boat."

"Can we get more ice cream first?" He polished off his cone. "I want to try the homemade ice cream now."

"Of course. Here, I'll help you carry your stuff." I leaned over to pick up his sewing machine.

"Good God, woman. Why do you have Michelle Obama arms?" he asked. "They're so defined, I hardly recognize the weakling library nerd I know and love."

"It's all those cast-iron pots," I grumped. "They're heavy."

"Well, it's working for you." He grabbed the hat box. "Come on, She-Ra, let's hit the bricks. Which way to the frozen milk-fat?"

"Follow me." I led the way down the sidewalk to downtown Camden Harbor. Before hitting the main drag, we passed the public beach and the CVS on the outskirts of downtown.

"Well, this is too effing cute!" Dev exclaimed as we hit Main Street. It really was. The last major downtown construction had been in 1885, so it still looked like a picture-perfect postcard full of whitewashed clapboard storefronts. The Dairy Bar was at the top of the street, next to the toy store.

"Thank God!" Dev burst through the door, raising his Ray-Bans. "I need more ice cream stat." He quickly scanned the giant chalkboard crowded with handwritten flavors. "So, I'm gonna need one scoop of Jamaica Me Nutty, one Café Mocha Chunk, one Rocky Rocky Road, and one Sticky Fractured Butterfingers, then top it all off with crushed Reese's, hot fudge, and M&M's. And whipped cream!" he concluded with a flourish.

"Wow." The girl behind the counter looked him up and down. "I don't know where you put it. I wish I had your metabolism!" She laughed.

"Wow, you are really pretty." Dev returned her once-over. "Like model-pretty. And I should know"—he leaned in conspiratorially—"I work for *Mode*."

I rolled my eyes.

"Oh my God." She blushed. "Not even! Thank you, though, that's so nice of you to say." She was really pretty. Dev was right—like model-pretty. Miles of limbs and flawless skin and shining mahogany hair that looked like it had escaped from a shampoo commercial. "Do you know what you want?" she asked me sweetly.

"Chocolate-chip cookie dough, please. Just the one scoop," I said, eyes on the mountain of ice cream the Scooper Girl had constructed for Dev.

Dev collected his enormous sundae. "I was starting to believe it was no longer possible for hot people to be nice. Ice Cream Scooper Girl has restored my faith in humanity." He took a huge bite of ice cream. *"Mmm."* He sighed euphorically. "I wanna live again! Oh God, I wanna live again! It really is a wonderful life! Thank you, Camden Harbor!"

"Come on, George Bailey, let's sit down." We paid and took seats at a small round table with two metal café chairs.

"Yum, yum, yum." Dev started working his way through the scoop of Jamaica Me Nutty.

"So, until the milk incident, how was the internship?"

"Shhp!" He threatened me with a plastic spoon. "We shall not speak of this until I've recovered from my post traumatic stress disorder. I need time."

"Too soon. Got it." I concentrated on finding all the cookie dough chunks in my ice cream.

"So, what's there to do for fun around here?" Dev asked. "Anything?"

"Um . . ." For a minute I was stumped. I mean, I thought Camden Harbor was lots of fun, but nothing that would be up Dev's alley was coming to mind. "Oh, wait!" Light bulb! Brilliant idea! "You'll love this, actually. There's a costume ball coming up! Pretty soon, actually."

"A costume ball? That does sound fun! Like Halloween? Ooh, I'll be a cowboy!"

"No, no, not that kind of costume," I explained. "Period costume. It's like a 1790s ball, and people even make their own clothes. Well, I'll probably rent, because I won't have time to work on anything, and it's in like two weeks, the first weekend in August—"

"Wait." Dev put down the spoon. "A sew-your-own colonial ball gown party?" I nodded. "Oh my GOD, be still my heart!" He clapped joyously. "I'm making you a dress." He started eating again.

"Oh, no, Dev, that's way too much work. I couldn't ask you to—"

"You didn't ask me to. I offered," he said simply. "So I'm doing it. Plus, how will I ever be a designer if I don't *design?*

If I don't get people out there wearing my label? I mean, yes, I wasn't planning on going into colonial couture, but every designer has to start somewhere, right?"

"I guess so."

"I can go too, right?" he asked.

"Of course." I mean, I didn't know if he was technically allowed to come, but I figured anyone in costume would be welcome. And if I knew Dev, he'd be dressed to the nines.

"Fantastic." Dev was almost done with his sundae. "Now, all we'll need is a fabric store . . ." he trailed off, looking around, like he was going to find a bolt of silk moiré in the Dairy Bar. "Hey! Gisele Bündchen!" No response. "I mean you, Scooper Girl." He sighed.

"Yeah?" She came to the edge of the counter.

"Do you know where the nearest fabric store is?" he asked.

"There's a So-Fro Fabric in Rockport. It's about a twenty-minute drive inland."

"A million times, thank you." He inclined his head in a half-bow, and she returned to whatever she was reading behind the counter. Dev's eyes suddenly lit up with fiery passion. "The flame of inspiration," he whispered. "I'm going to make you an exact replica of Keira Knightley's wedding dress in *The Duchess*. Except not in that icky yellow. You'd look totally washed out. Maybe blue . . ." He sighed dreamily.

"Um, Dev, are you psychotic?"

"No, of course not. You know I only take my Paxil recreationally."

"I saw *The Duchess*. Three times, actually."

"*Lame,*" Dev coughed.

"Shut up. What I meant was that dress is *insane*. The costumes in that movie are so elaborate, they're out of control! They're amazingly, heart-stoppingly, breathtakingly beautiful, but there's no way you could do that in this amount of time! It's impossible!"

"Libby"—he took my hands, eyes shining—"impossible things are happening every day. Trust me. I can do this. I need to do this. This will be my finest moment. My greatest triumph. I am a caterpillar, Libby, a caterpillar about to become a butterfly," he whispered passionately. "Let me fly, Libby. Let me spread my wings and fly."

"Okay, Dev, fly." I sighed.

"Yay!!!"

"Only one problem," I said.

"What?"

"A twenty-minute *drive* inland? I don't have a car."

"A minor detail." He waved his hand. "I'm sure you know someone who does. You get the car, Libby, and I'll get you the dress of your dreams. We just need that fabric fast."

"Okay." I set my jaw determinedly. "I'll get that car."

"I have no doubts."

Who did I know with a car? None of the interns . . . I knew Garrett had one, but I really didn't want to have to ask him for a favor. Maybe Cam had one . . . I'd ask, and then Garrett would be a last resort—only in case of an absolute emergency.

"I'm done." Dev put his spoon in his empty cup. "Can we go to the boat? I want to start sketching."

"Of course." We threw out our cups and headed outside, walking back to the museum.

"Damn." Dev squinted into the setting sun. "Check out how hot that guy is. The one running. Over there."

"Where?" I followed his pointing finger. "Oh, perfect!" I waved. "Hey! Hey, Cam! Over here!"

"You know him?" Dev's jaw dropped. "Oh my God, you do not seriously know him!"

"Seriously, I do."

Cam, shirtless, jogged over to meet us. "Hey, babe."

Dev mouthed, "Babe?!"

"I'd hug you, but I'm all sweaty." He grinned.

"Yes, you are," Dev said breathily.

Cam shot him a weird look.

"Cam, this is Dev," I introduced him. "Dev's my best friend from home. He's visiting me for a while."

"Why hellooooo." Dev extended his hand.

Cam shook it for the briefest of seconds, before dropping it like a red hot poker.

"I don't have cooties," Dev muttered under his breath.

"We just had ice cream!" I said brightly, trying to diffuse the mounting tension.

"What?" Cam snapped. "Where?" he asked anxiously.

"Um . . . the Dairy Bar." Why was he tweaking out?"

"The Dairy Bar," he said nervously, looking over my head toward the Dairy Bar. "You did, huh? How was that?"

"Um . . . fine?"

"Listen, I really have to run," Cam said, still acting all shifty. "I have to, um, keep my heart rate up."

"Okay." I tried to catch his eye, but he was still looking over my head. "Hey, listen, Cam, before you go, do you have a car?"

"Naw, Libs, I have the boat, you know that. I can't afford

both." He started jogging. "Later!" He disappeared off into the direction of the museum.

"Uh, you should tell Homophobe Hottie that 'gay' isn't contagious." Dev lowered his sunglasses. "And how did he even know I was gay?" he demanded.

"You're wearing Armani Exchange white jeans and a doodle-print Marc Jacobs T-shirt in a town where Dockers are considered the height of fashion and the only designer people can name is L.L.Bean."

"Hmph," Dev snorted. "Point taken."

Weighed down by the sewing machine, we made our way back to the museum at a glacial place, gossiping as we went along and stopping so Dev could take iPhone pictures of everything he thought was cute. By the time we finally hit the museum grounds, night had fallen.

"And here she is." I gestured grandly. "The *Lettie Mae Howell*! Home, sweet home!"

"I cannot believe you live on a boat." Dev followed me up the gangplank. "That is so effing weird. Who are you, Captain Hook?"

"Lots of cool people live on boats," I countered, sewing machine banging against my knees as we went down the steps into the belly of the ship. "Like, um, Vikings. Vikings are totally badass."

"I am not even going to dignify that with a response."

"Okay, give me a minute, I'll think of someone cool. Like—"

I froze. Dev bumped into me, looked over my shoulder, and then screamed like a little girl. I joined him.

"AAAAAAAAAAAAAAAY!!!!!!!!!!!!!!!"

The ghost was standing at the end of the passageway that led to the galley. It was completely motionless. Dev, however, turned and ran for his life.

"What's going on?" Garrett burst out of the fo'c's'le.

"Ghost! Garrett! GHOST!" I shrieked. He ran back into the fo'c's'le, returned with his video camera, and skidded to a stop in front of me.

"Is that a purse? It's kind of bulky," he asked, befuddled.

"No, you idiot, it's a sewing machine! Go!" I shooed him away.

Garrett chased the ghost down toward the galley.

"I see it, Libby, I see it!" he shouted excitedly. "I've got it on film!"

"Awesome!" I cheered, and ran into the galley. Running *toward* the ghost? There must have been something wrong with me. By the time I got there, Garrett was standing alone in the galley.

"It's gone," he said breathlessly. "But look, Libby, *look.*" Grinning from ear to ear, he played back a fifteen-second shot on the screen. It was fuzzy but distinctly there—the ghostly sailor, all in white.

"Oh my God, that's amazing!" I clutched his arm, and we jumped up and down.

"This is huge, Libby. *Huge.*" He couldn't stop grinning. "I'm getting so close to figuring this out! And now I know it's definitely a person. Not a hologram. Which was, admittedly, a stupid theory, but—"

"Oh, shoot! Dev!" I remembered suddenly. He was probably halfway to Rhode Island by now. "Garrett, I've gotta find my friend."

PILGRIMS DON'T WEAR PINK

"Who?" He looked confused.

"Oh, my friend from home is on the run from an international publishing conglomerate with designs on his life, so I'm hiding him in Camden Harbor," I explained, mounting the stairs to the deck.

"You are certainly . . . one of a kind, Libby Kelting." He shook his head in disbelief. "Wait. I'll help you find him. Let me get a flashlight."

I smiled. Not just because Garrett had caught the ghost on film, but because it seemed like things were finally back to normal. We ran onto the dark grounds of the museum, Garrett scanning the grass with the beam of his flashlight.

"Dev!" I called. "Dev! Dev!" Garrett took up the call as well.

A soft "Oh, no" floated in from somewhere.

"Wait! Quiet! Shhh!" I listened intently.

Yep, it was there. Faint. And sort of echoey. But there. "Oh, no, I do not hook up, up, I go slow."

"Kelly Clarkson!" I cried triumphantly. "Dev's happy place!" Garrett still looked confused. "He's around here somewhere."

I ran, following the sound, and it led me to a barrel. I stuck my head in.

"Hi, Dev."

He was curled up in a ball in the bottom of the barrel, hugging his knees to his chest and rocking back and forth.

"Why didn't you tell me?" he whispered in anguish.

"I *did* tell you!" I protested. "You just didn't believe me!"

"Libby? Hey, Libby! Where are you?" Garrett shouted.

"Who's that?" Dev asked.

"That's my bunkmate, Garrett."

"Ooh-ooh," Dev singsonged. Even traumatized, he could tease me.

"Oh, stop, it is *not like that*. He's pretty much hideous."

"What, like Spencer Pratt post–facial hair? Or like a mole man in the *National Enquirer*?"

"What? No, neither." God, Dev's mind must have been a strange place. "He looks . . . fine. He's not like ugly or anything." I thought about it for a minute. "Not ugly at all, actually." I mean he certainly wasn't hot, but he wasn't unattractive. I could see how someone might find him attractive. Not that I did. Because I didn't. But I could see how someone could. "I meant personality."

"What, he's an asshole?"

"No, no, he's nice. Mostly." I wasn't explaining this at all well. "Just, um, annoying."

"Okay." Dev shot me a funny look.

"Hello, Kitty." Garrett had found us. "Back in the barrel?"

I popped my head out. "Hi. I found Dev. Help me get him out?"

"I understand why you guys are friends." He chuckled.

Garrett joined me at the barrel, and together we extracted Dev.

"Hey, man" — Garrett extended his hand — "I'm Garrett."

"Nice to meet you." Dev dusted himself off and shook Garrett's hand. "Now can someone get me the eff off of Haunted Hill here? Is there a non–Bates Motel in this Yankee *Deliverance*?"

"Yeah, I can give you a ride to the Sea Breeze Motel, if you want. It's clean," Garrett offered.

"Thanks, I — wait — you have a car?"

"Uh, yeah. That's why I offered to give you a ride."

"Screw the motel. Can you take me to the So-Fro Fabric in Rockport?"

"Oh, Dev, Garrett probably doesn't want to do that, and it's probably closed by now anyway, and—"

"I don't mind." Garrett shrugged. "And it's open till ten."

"Road trip!" Dev cheered. *"Vamanos!"*

"Okay, Dora the Explorer, cool your jets," I grumbled. The three of us walked toward the parking lot, Garrett leading the way. Dev raised his eyebrows at the myriad *Battlestar Galactica,* World of Warcraft, *Star Wars,* and *Star Trek* bumper stickers plastered to the back of Garrett's car. I rolled my eyes in response. We all piled into Garrett's old Toyota, me riding shotgun, Dev in the back.

"Oh, no, you did *not* let Libby pick the music," Dev moaned as we pulled onto the road.

"I didn't. This is my CD," Garrett said.

"Really?" Dev gawped. "This is the song Libby listens to when she's sad."

I turned to glare at him and shake my head. "TMI," I hissed. Garrett didn't need to know that we actually had something in common.

"I wouldn't have picked you for a Radiohead girl." Garrett smoothly turned the wheel with one hand.

"I love this song." I looked out the window, so I wouldn't have to look at him. "In the deepest ocean, the bottom of the sea," I sang softly.

Garrett sang-spoke, "Your eyes, they turn me," never really finding any discernible key, but turning it into a kind of spoken-word poetry.

I caught a glimpse of Dev in the mirror's reflection. His eyebrows were waggling so furiously, it looked like he was trying to communicate something in semaphore. Semaphore was not, unfortunately, covered in our brief maritime orientation.

After my refusal to answer any of his eyebrow-semaphore questions, Dev launched into a long explanation about the ball and Keira Knightley's *Duchess* wedding dress and pin tucks.

"I'll make you something too," he offered Garrett.

"Oh, uh, you don't have to do that. I probably won't even go . . ."

"Um, helloooo, you *have* to go! It's a *ball!* You're going." Garrett tried to object. "Tut-tut!" Dev scolded him. "Don't bother arguing. You're going. I decided."

Dev always got his way. This was no exception, and Garrett looked resigned to his fate. Soon after, we pulled into the So-Fro Fabric.

"Amuse yourselves." Dev rocketed out of the car. "I have full creative control, so don't bother picking anything out. I've got it covered." He practically skipped into the store, and we followed, slightly less giddy.

Garrett wandered around, clearly bored out of his mind but being a good sport about it. I joined Dev in the "Special Occasion Fabrics" aisle.

"Blue," he said confidently. "Definitely blue. I just need to find the right texture . . ." He wandered up and down the aisles, stroking fabrics. "He's kind of cute."

"What? Who? Garrett?" I asked, surprised.

"Super-nerd, obviously. But you're into that, so—"

"Into what?"

"Huge into nerd."

"No, I'm not. I—"

"Don't try to deny it. Fact." He fingered a bolt of blue shot silk. "But I think he's a secret hot nerd. Like Seth, on the *O.C.* No one thought he was going to be hot, because he was all like ooh, Death Cab for Cutie! Comic books! But then he was. H-O-T-T hot." We leaned around the aisle to peek at Garrett, who had bent over to pick up a few bolts of fabric he'd accidentally knocked over. "Definitely secret hot nerd," Dev said confidently.

"You're crazy." I shook my head. A nerd? Definitely. Secret hot? Doubtful. "I'm going to go play with the buttons."

Dev worked pretty quickly. After one loop around the store, he had made his decisions, and before we knew it, we were headed back home to Camden Harbor.

"Drop me off at the Sea Breeze Motel, please," Dev requested politely.

"Dev, are you sure?" I turned around to look at him.

"I am *not* staying on Satan's ship. Let me out right up here." Garrett pulled into the motel parking lot.

"Do you have money? Are you sure you're okay? How are you going to—"

"Stop worrying, Libby." He hopped out of the car, sewing machine, hat box, and shopping bags in hand. "You've restored my faith in humanity and given me a purpose in life. Mono Corps be damned. I'll make it work." He slammed the door shut and strode confidently toward the lobby.

"Make it work." I smiled. "And they say you can't learn anything from reality TV."

I turned up the music, and we drove back to the ship.

chapter ten

The weeks leading up the ball seemed to fly by at the speed of light. It was like the anticipation plus the time pressure of finishing our costumes had combined with that terrible end-of-summer feeling to create some kind of ultra-speedy time warp. The end of July was a whirlwind of patterns, cutting, sewing, quilting, and trimming. I spent my days trying desperately to help the girls finish their quilting projects and my nights at the motel assisting Dev with his "colonial couture." Dev had arranged to stay at the Sea Breeze for free, in exchange for promising to update all the maids' uniforms once the ball was over. Patches of fabric and little silver needles danced before my eyes when I tried to sleep.

Garrett had been in a remarkably good mood, having managed to parlay his second ghost sighting (with video, this time!) into another smashingly successful article. It had been picked up by several other Maine newspapers, including the three papers with the largest circulation: the *Bangor Daily News,* the *Lewiston Sun Journal,* and the *Portland Press Herald.* Even better, it had traveled down south to a small paragraph in the "Special Reports" section of the *Boston Globe,* which was, as Garrett reminded me about fifty times a day, the fourteenth most widely read paper in the United States.

While Garrett was out of his mind with glee, the paranormal societies were just straight up out of their minds. They had gone nuts after discovering Garrett now had what they considered video proof of paranormal activity. (Garrett, of course, thought of it as video proof that a very corporeal someone was up to no good.) The Paranormal Enthusiasts of Maine were sticking to their original plan of petitioning President Harrow, only now, in addition to their 24/7 sit-in, they had added megaphones. Yes, megaphones. Mostly they chanted a nonstop chorus of "What do we want? Onto the boat! When do we want it? Now!"—although occasionally they would read various treatises on cruelty to unhappy spirits and our duty, nay, our privilege as fellow humans to help them cross over to a better place in the beyond.

The BAGS Ghost Slayers, however, still hadn't processed that neither Garrett nor I had the authority to let them onto the ship. So they had redoubled their efforts to get on our good side. First, Beardy sent us "Just for Fun!" balloon bouquets: Garrett's featured frolicking sea creatures and jewel-tone balloons, whereas mine was all pastels and a giant silver "PRINCESS" crown. I brought them all into the fo'c's'le to try to liven the place up a bit. It certainly was feeling a lot cheerier, albeit a bit claustrophobic, until Garrett had a horrible clown nightmare and attacked them, popping them all in his sleep. The giant stuffed panda and the "We Love You Bear-y Much" teddy met similar unpleasant fates.

I thought the gifts were a bit much, but the Ghost Slayers were panicking: Sally Minich, local reporter for MWTW News Channel 8, had recently shown up to express her interest in airing the video clip. And as the Ghost Slayers also had a TV show, they had similar designs on the prize.

Beardy was halfway up the gangplank with a "You're So

Special!" Daisy Smiley Face Cookie BouTray when he discovered Garrett had done the unthinkable and given the video to MWTW News 8. Beardy angrily stuffed as many cookies as possible in his mouth before dumping the rest in the water for the seagulls to feast on.

So even though there were no more inappropriate gift baskets coming our way, Garrett was still pretty pleased. He didn't even complain when Dev had accidentally stuck him with pins about fifteen times during his fitting. Nor did he complain when Dev dragged him back to the motel for a second fitting, and I knew that Garrett wasn't exactly gung ho on the whole costume thing.

Nevertheless, against all the odds, before I knew it Garrett was waiting, fully dressed, in the lobby of the Sea Breeze Motel, while Dev and I put the finishing touches on our outfits in his room.

"Dev, I underestimated you."

"I know," he said smugly, tying on my choker. "There!" He walked to the front and examined me with his quizzing glass, which is what gentlemen of fashion called monocles back in the 1790s. Much to my surprise, Dev had actually done research and spent hours poring over fashion history books. He'd decided we were much too stylish to dress like simple colonial Americans and had instead outfitted us like British fashion plates. Dev looked like the Scarlet Pimpernel, every inch a dandy in a high-collared embroidered velvet jacket in rich plum, ornate brocade waistcoat, lacy cravat that tumbled like a waterfall, and fawn knee breeches so tight they bordered on the obscene. "I have truly outdone myself this time."

"You have," I agreed fervently. It seemed impossible that he had created something so amazing in two weeks in a tiny motel room. The dress was astonishing—a large panniered overskirt on top of a heavily embroidered, hand-embellished stomacher, and an underskirt decorated with swoops and tucks. The sleeves came tightly down to my elbows before exploding into froths of silk and lace and exposing strings of faux-pearl bracelets at my wrists. It looked exactly like the one in *The Duchess,* except in a beautiful periwinkle blue silk.

"That color makes your eyes look effing enormous!" Dev said happily. "Your boobs are pretty effing enormous too."

"Dev, we were having a nice moment!" I admonished him. "But now that the moment's been ruined, let's go—I don't want to miss the Scottish reel."

"Now, now, now, wait just a minute." Dev pulled out a box from under the bed. "Cinderella needs one more thing before she's ready to go to the ball." He opened the box. "Choos."

I looked inside. Cream Jimmy Choo slingbacks with slightly pointed toes and a Swarovski crystal buckle. They looked exactly like a modern update of an eighteenth-century dancing slipper, diamond buckles and all.

"Oh, Dev." I gasped with disbelief. "How did you—"

"I'm your fairy godfather, darling! I couldn't let you leave without your glass slippers!" He looked around, then whispered naughtily, "I stole them for you from the sample closet at grown-up *Mode.*"

"Mono Corps really is going to kill you," I said as I slipped them on. "Oh, they fit perfectly," I murmured with a sigh.

"You're my best friend, Libby. I'd risk death for you any day." He smiled. "If they'd made them in a men's size ten, you'd have been shit out of luck, though, obviously."

"Obviously," I agreed. "And just so you know, you are the most fabulous fop I've ever seen." I kissed him on the cheek. In the seventeenth century, *fop* had been a derogatory term for men who were way too into fashion. But Dev was more like an end of the eighteenth-century fictional fop—like Sir Percy Blakeney, the Scarlet Pimpernel, using his foppishness to disguise hidden depths and liberate French prisoners from the guillotine. Or to liberate Choos from a sample closet. "And I mean that in the best possible way."

"Why, thank you, my dear. Might as well just stick a feather in my hat and call it macaroni."

"Dev!" I started to tear up. "You really *do* know your fashion history!" A *macaroni* was the mid- to late eighteenth-century term for the most outlandishly affected, fashion-obsessed, exquisite fops in existence. It came from the Macaroni Club, an elite group of flashy young men who'd traveled to Italy, which was then, as always, the fashion mecca. That's what "Yankee Doodle" is about—making fun of how Americans were so sartorially challenged, they thought just putting a feather in your hat was enough to make you a macaroni. As if. No, you had to be over the top to the utmost. No wonder the look suited Dev to a T.

He blushed modestly and cleared his throat. "And now, Cinderella, your carriage awaits! Well, our Toyota awaits," he corrected himself, and shut the door behind us as we crossed into the hall. "And above all else, remember this—if you don't stay out past midnight, I'll effing kill you," he warned.

"I don't think that's how the story goes."

"Please. I don't know what that bibbidi-bobbidi-bitch was on about. No self-respecting fairy leaves a party before four."

We hit the lobby. Garrett was sitting on a coffee-stained couch, flipping through a "Maine: The Vacationland!" brochure, looking totally out of place under the flickering fluorescent lighting.

"Libby!" He sprang to his feet, banging a knee on the coffee table. "You look — I — you — uh — I — oh — wow —"

"I've rendered a man speechless." Dev nodded with satisfaction. "My work here is done." He exited the Sea Breeze dramatically and sailed into the parking lot.

"You look very nice, Garrett." He really looked much better out of those stupid T-shirts and endless parade of cargo shorts. His was a simple navy suit with a pale yellow striped waistcoat and cotton cravat. Actually . . . I looked more closely. I suddenly realized why it looked familiar. It was an exact replica of one of the suits worn by Dominic Cooper, the love interest in *The Duchess*. (I know, I know, I've seen that movie way too many times.) I made a quick mental note to have a chat with Dev later about fashion matchmaking. Regardless, it suited him. "Awkward and uncomfortable, but nice."

"Shhh!" Garrett glanced worriedly out to where Dev was. "I don't want him to know that I don't really like all this costume stuff. He worked really hard, and he's really good. I just feel stupid. But that's my problem. Not his. So I don't want him to know."

"Your secret's safe with me," I said, patting his arm. "Let's go."

We piled into the car. My dress took up the entire passenger seat. On the plus side, if we crashed, I wouldn't even need an air bag.

"I love dancing!" Dev trilled. "I'm so excited."

"Me too," I admitted. Sure, it was a Toyota, not a coach, but I really *did* feel like Cinderella. I mean, I had spent the afternoon sweeping out the hearth, after all.

"Just dance, gonna be okay," Dev sang. "Da-da doo-doo-mmm, just dance."

"I wouldn't get your hopes up for any Lady Gaga," I warned him. "It's a string quartet."

"Maybe they take requests," he said hopefully. "Da-da doo-doo-mmm."

It was such a short trip, we probably could have walked from the Sea Breeze instead of driven, but I don't think any of us wanted to walk down Main Street in our ball gear. Well, except for Dev, maybe. Once he'd parked the car, Garrett came around to the passenger door to help pull me out of the car. It was definitely a two-man job. But I managed to make it out from under all my layers of fabric, and we walked to the ball.

The ball was being held at the Manor House, which was the biggest, grandest house in the museum's collection. A stately white pillared mansion at the edge of the museum grounds, it had an actual ballroom inside, as well as a terrace and a formal French garden out back. Apparently, the museum made a large portion of its revenue renting it out for weddings. But tonight it was all ours.

"OMG. Loves it!" Dev shrieked at the top of his lungs as he bounded up the steps. I walked up a little more slowly, careful to do nothing to injure my shoes. Footmen were posted at the door, and they ushered us through the foyer to the ballroom.

The room was huge, golden, and glowing with a thousand electric candle lights. Crystal chandeliers and gold filigree sparkled all along the walls, and the ceiling was covered in a cherubic mural. The room was packed with women in silks and satins, and straight-backed men in suits. Finally, I felt like I'd found my time machine.

"How beautiful." I sighed happily and turned to Garrett. "This is everything I ever dreamed of."

"A bunch of historians playing dress-up?" he teased.

"No, you idiot." I smacked him lightly. "This . . . this lost world, this other time that I thought I'd only ever read about or see in movies. But now I feel like I'm really here. Somewhere impossible."

"And how does it measure up?"

I looked up at him. "It's better than I imagined."

"Let's dance!" Dev shimmied. "Come on, come on, let's tear it up in here! We're gonna party like it's 1799! Woot woot!"

"Ooh, yes please." I took his hand. "Garrett? You coming?"

"Uh, no." He adjusted his glasses. "Definitely not dancing."

"Oh, come on, don't be lame," I wheedled. "Maybe later?"

"Maybe later," he agreed, but I sort of doubted he meant it.

"Well, I can't wait for later!" Dev cried. "Away we go!"

Dev and I hopped onto the end of some sort of reel-type dance, as Garrett went off, probably in search of the punch bowl or something equally antisocial. Neither Dev nor I really had any idea what we were doing, but we tried to follow the rest of the couples. And as always, we compensated for our lack of skills with enthusiasm and flair.

"Jazz hands, Libby! Jazz hands!" Dev shouted during a rigadoon. Yes, we certainly had a style all our own. Three minuets

later I was almost ready to see if I could coax Garrett into dancing, when . . .

"You!" Ashling shrieked, barreling down on me, every
flounce on her beribboned ball gown aquiver with rage, and
towing a skinny, gangly guy in glasses. "Look what your influ-
ence has wrought!"

I followed her pointing finger to the corner of the ballroom,
where Suze and the Dread Pirate Travis, for once not looking
ridiculous but rather very dashing in his costume, were vigorously making out.

"Awesome!" I shouted. "You go, girl!" Yeah, I can't pull that
off. But I meant it.

"This is all your fault!" she said.

"I wish I could take credit for this, but I really had nothing
to do with it." This was so out of left field, I think the only
person to blame was Cupid. That sneaky little devil.

"Princess, can we please dance this minuet?" the gangly guy
interrupted.

"Why, Martin Cheeseman, as I live and breathe!" I exclaimed with delight. "I was beginning to think you were a
myth!" It must have been him. I mean, who else could it have
been?

"No, I am no mythological beast! Neither nymph nor satyr
I, merely a mortal LARPer," he said with a grin.

"LARPer?" I asked.

"Live Action Role Play," he explained excitedly. "Oh, you'll
like this. Working at a living history museum and all. And
we're always looking for more girls! Have you heard of the Al-
liance? We are one of the largest medieval live-action fantasy
role-play games in the Americas, dedicated to recreating the

Days of Legend as we would like them, not as they actually were, per se —"

"*What* did I tell you about talking to *her?*" Ashling hissed.

"But, princess . . ."

"We're going. Now," she snapped, and dragged him away. Martin Cheeseman waved at me as he disappeared into the crowd. Poor guy. He seemed pretty nice. Dev had run away the minute Ashling showed up, still slightly shell-shocked from his stint on the steps, so I was now surrounded by strangers. I scanned the crowd, wondering if I could coax Garrett into dancing now. But the only person I recognized was Neil, two heads taller than everyone else, doing a stately gavotte with one of the marine biologists. To get a better view, I climbed the first several steps of the grand staircase leading up to the second floor of the house and looked out over the revelers.

A telltale whistle caught my attention.

"Well, get a load of you." Cam whistled again. "Libs, you take my breath away." He bowed, then walked up to join me at the foot of the stairs. Devastatingly handsome as always, he was dressed as a naval officer, in a navy jacket with epaulets and red trim. A tricorn hat with red, white, and blue cockades perched at a rakish angle on his thick blond hair. More so than ever, he was Prince Charming come to life. If I hadn't felt like Cinderella before, I sure did now. I stepped down to the bottom step, and he kissed my hand. "Care to join me for a turn around the garden?" he asked as he offered his arm gallantly.

"Oh, can we dance first?" I asked.

"Come on, don't you want to see the garden?"

"Well, of course, but maybe we could go later? Like when the quartet is taking a break?" I suggested.

"Libs, I need to talk to you," he said, eyes shining sincerely. "It's really important."

"Well . . . okay," I acquiesced. "If it's really important." He did look really concerned.

"It is." He took my arm and led me out to the garden.

The large French doors that led from the ballroom to the terrace were open. A few people milled around the flagstones, clutching punch glasses and laughing softly. Cam led me off the steps, away from the terrace, and down a hedgerow.

"Somewhere . . . a little more private," he muttered distractedly.

We took a turn and ended up in an abandoned patch of shrubbery, where Cam promptly stuck his tongue down my throat.

"What are you doing?" I pushed him off, surprised. What was going on? He'd said he wanted to talk. And I still wanted to dance.

"Come on, Libs, you know what I'm doing."

"You said we needed to talk." I pushed my hands against his chest, keeping him at arm's length.

"Isn't this more fun than talking?" he asked mischievously, and tried to kiss me again.

"Seriously, Cam." I turned my face away. "Let's go back inside. I want to dance."

"No!" he said harshly, grabbing my wrist.

"Ow, Cam, stop, you're holding too tight."

"Then stop fighting me and *come here,*" he said imperiously, all traces of playfulness gone from his voice. When I tried to pull away, he yanked me back into him and kissed me roughly.

"Cam, seriously, get off of me!" As we struggled, I toppled

out of my left shoe. Breaking free, I abandoned the shoe and ran unevenly through the damp grass, hobbling deeper into the garden. In any circumstances, Cam was much faster than me, and now that I was minus one shoe, he caught up almost instantly.

"Stop playing hard to get, Libby." He grabbed my arms so tightly, I could feel bruises forming.

"I'm not playing hard to get! Please, Cam, please let me go. You're hurting me," I whimpered.

"Libby! Libby! Are you all right?" Garrett called from somewhere in the distance. "I found your shoe!"

"Come on, you've been practically *begging* for it all summer, running around in those slutty outfits —"

"That was my uniform! For my job! That wasn't me — that was all Roger!" I said desperately.

"Yeah, okay, sure." Cam rolled his eyes. "I don't know who you think you're fooling. I know you want it."

"Don't you dare talk to her like that." Garrett appeared from behind shrubbery, cradling my shoe, followed closely by Dev.

"Oh, come on, man, can you just be cool, for once?" Cam said. "Seriously, can you not cock-block me right now?"

"Okay, that's it," Garrett said angrily, taking off his jacket. "Let's go."

"'Let's go? Let's go?'" Cam parroted, laughing. "You have got to be kidding." He smirked. "What are you gonna do? You're such a pussy. Come on, look at you. You've finally found your people — a girl and a fag."

BAM! My fist collided with Cam's nose, which erupted in a fountain of blood.

"Nobody calls my friend a fag," I said fiercely, wiping the blood off my knuckles.

"I think you broke my fucking nose!" Cam shrieked, sounding eerily similar to Marcia Brady.

"I *hope* I broke your fucking nose!" I shouted back.

"Libby, you punched someone!" Dev squealed in delighted disbelief.

"I know, and it really hurt my hand," I whispered so only Dev could hear.

"Aren't you glad I made you take that women's self-defense workshop for your PE requirement?" Dev whispered back.

I fervently nodded my agreement. "He's just lucky I didn't jam his nose up into his brain and kill him instantly."

"We should all be so lucky," Dev said, glaring at Cam.

"I can't have a broken nose. It'll ruin my face." Cam started to cry, then ran off back to the Manor House, presumably in search of a first-aid kit.

"I have *got* to see this!" Dev followed him gleefully.

Garrett and I were left alone in the garden.

"Wow." He shook his head in disbelief. "I'm sure as hell gonna think twice before making another Hello Kitty crack." He shook his head again, still stunned. "You know, I was, uh, gonna punch him."

"I'm sure you were." I smiled reassuringly. "I just did it first."

"Here." He knelt down, shoe still in hand, and slid it onto my foot. A perfect fit.

Suddenly everything was clear. Maybe Prince Charming just *looked* charming and wasn't charming at all. Maybe he was just a cocky asshole with a crown and a boat. Maybe Cinderella

—who was, after all, just a hearth-sweeping baker with a weakness for nice shoes—would be happier with the sarcastic nerd who liked Cinderella not just dressed to the nines at a ball, but even covered in ashes and upside down in a barrel. After all, it was the nerd who'd found Cinderella's Choo. And if the Choo fits . . .

"I can't believe I fell for that idiot." I shook my head.

"Oh, I can," Garrett said grimly, rising to his feet. "Let me guess . . . he quoted some Shakespeare at you, brought you flowers, and swept you off your feet with all the romantic bullshit you always dreamed of but were afraid only existed in books?"

"Um, yeah, actually. Pretty much exactly." Because that was it. I hadn't liked him just because he was cute—it was all the Shakespeare, the flowers, the chivalry. All the romance I'd spent my whole life searching for. "How did you know?"

"Last year Cam, uh, slept with my girlfriend." Garrett cleared his throat. "Well, ex-girlfriend now."

"Jesus, Garrett." I looked up at him and was stunned by how handsome he was. How had I not noticed that before? I mean, he wasn't perfect. Far from it. But he was better than perfect. Because he was just . . . Garrett. I reached, tentatively, for his hand. He let me take it. "Why didn't you *tell* me this?"

"It's, uh, not exactly my favorite topic for discussion."

"Well, okay, yeah, understandable, but I was sort of *dating* the guy. I would have appreciated a heads-up."

"I kind of thought you'd figure it out yourself, Libby." He shrugged. "You're really smart."

"Clearly, not that smart," I muttered, still mad at myself.

"And I didn't think you'd believe me if I told you Cam was screwing every attractive girl from here to Millinocket," he added.

"The scooper!" It hit me like a lightning bolt. That's why Cam was being all tweaky outside the Dairy Bar. And why he hustled us away from that girl in the bikini on the beach. And why the Squaddies thought my name was Kelly. Or Melissa. God, he really must have been screwing every girl in Maine aged eighteen to twenty-five. Garrett was looking at me like I was nuts. Right, Libby, focus. "Why wouldn't I believe you?" I asked curiously.

"Talking shit about the guy who's involved with the girl you like? Yeah, that's credible," he said sarcastically.

"You—you like me?" I asked cautiously. "I mean, still?"

"Libby, I've liked you since the minute you geeked out and started talking about *Northanger Abbey*," he admitted. "I've never stopped. I mean, how could I *not* like you?" He smiled shyly. "You're . . . you're . . ." He shook his head and thought hard. "Indescribable," he said finally. "I can't put it into words. I mean, you know enough about colonial America to host your own History Channel show; you can out-sing Beyoncé; you bake like you're from another world . . . seriously. I had a piece of that pie on the Fourth of July, and it was unreal. And the way your face lights up when you talk about the things you love? Your passion for history and books and . . . It's amazing. I've never seen anything like it. I've never met anyone like you. I feel like every day I learn something new about you, and every day you surprise me. I never know what to expect. Is there anything you *can't* do?" He laughed. "You're like Wonder Woman." He picked up my wrists, where the little strings of pearls jangled. "Indestructible bracelets and all. Fighting crime, chasing ghosts, throwing punches." He moved his hands from my wrists to hold my hands. "If I hadn't seen your Hello Kitty underwear, I might think you were superhuman. But I'm pretty sure superheroes don't wear Hello Kitty underwear."

For a moment I was speechless. I mean, sure, I knew some of those things were true—but I'd never really thought about myself like that. Like I was that special or anything. But the way Garrett was looking down at me, eyes shining, I almost felt like I *was* Wonder Woman. Like I was invincible. It was like he was the first person who had really seen me, and seen the best possible me—and here I was thinking all summer that he was a geeky jerk who just happened to be a great kisser. How had I been so blind?

"Oh, I'm—I'm not Wonder Woman," I muttered finally, blushing. "Far from it. I mean, if anything, I'm like . . . Stupid Girl."

"Stupid Girl?" He raised an eyebrow. "I don't think she was in the Justice League."

"Argh, shut up. So I don't know anything about comic books or superheroes. You know what I mean." I turned red again, grateful that it was dark enough that he probably couldn't tell just how furiously I was blushing. "I'm trying to apologize here. Because I was an idiot." He raised the other eyebrow. "Not just because I fell for someone as fake as Cam, but even worse because I totally misjudged you."

"*You* misjudged *me?*" He smirked. "Miss Practically Perfect Kelting?"

"Don't you dare gloat." I smiled back. "I'm trying to say I was wrong. About you. About everything, really. I assumed you were a jerk, because, oh, I don't know, you left me in that barrel, and you weren't exactly excited to have me on the boat, and you kept calling me Nancy Drew, and I kept thinking you were all pompous and self-important and—"

"Are you going to get to any of my good parts anytime soon?" He laughed.

"No, no, that's what I'm saying!" I protested. "You have so many good parts. I mean, you're funny and smart and kind, and I have so much fun when I'm with you, and I really admire the way you go after what you want . . . I mean the way that you talked yourself onto the boat to write the story? That took guts. As does ghost chasing, in my opinion, because it's really scary down there. And I've read your articles. You're a really good writer, Garrett. Really talented. But you're so much more than all of that, I mean you're . . . you're . . . indescribable." He smiled as I echoed his earlier words. "For way too long, I looked at you, and I saw . . . all the wrong things." I shook my head. "I couldn't see past the Cylon T-shirt to what was underneath."

"There's nothing wrong with Cylons," he interrupted.

"I know." I placed my hand on his chest. "That's exactly what I'm saying. I don't know what a Cylon is, but I love that you love them. Because that's part of what makes you . . . you."

Garrett leaned down to kiss me. It wasn't the Fourth of July anymore, yet the fireworks were there all the same.

chapter eleven

I didn't just make it through the end of Girls of Long Ago Camp—I *floated* through the end of Girls of Long Ago Camp. I was sort of a disaster, putting salt in the sugar and sugar in the salt, but I was so happy, I didn't care. I walked around smiling all day long, pretty much completely and utterly useless.

Eventually, the girls couldn't take it anymore.

"Miss Libby, why are you so happy?" Robin asked suspiciously, as I put together everyone's veritable mountain of needlepoint Souvenirs of Long Ago, including the quilting project that had miraculously come together at the last minute.

"Well, Robin"—I handed over her stack of samplers and quilt—"it turns out Nick Jonas was right."

"I knew it," she said smugly. "The Jonas Brothers are never wrong." As she moved to wait in the hallway with the rest of the girls who'd already gotten their stuff, she sang, "Everyone knows it's meant to be, falling in love, just you and me . . ."

Emily came up next. "Now, Miss Libby, don't forget to send my dad the recipe," she reminded me for the millionth time as she rearranged my stack to make it lay neater. "As a PDF file, not a Word document, okay?"

"I got it, Em. I don't actually live in the eighteenth century, remember?"

"Hmm." She looked down her nose at me through her glasses.

Crazy as it was, the recipe for Miss Libby's Colonial Caramel Apple Pie was going to be appearing in an issue of *Bon Appétit* coming soon to a newsstand near you, the centerpiece of a four-page spread on early American desserts. My faith in Mono Corps International had been somewhat restored.

"Goodbye, Mith Libby," Amanda said sadly as she walked up to get her stuff.

"Oh, Scarecrow," I said, hugging her. "I think I'll miss you most of all."

"Why am I a tharecrow?"

"Never mind." I patted her head. "Let's go to the Welcome Center, one last time."

I couldn't believe camp was over. I'd be back in the Bromleigh Homestead the next day, to clean everything up and get it ready for normal museum viewing once again. But without the pack of gigglers I'd come to know and love, it just wouldn't be the same. After lots of hugs and a few tearful goodbyes, all the girls had been returned to their parents, to go home to their lives of Twitter and *Twilight*. But maybe, hopefully, somewhere along the way, I'd created a few future historians.

Smiling somewhat wistfully, I made my way quickly back to the homestead, eager to change so I could get back to the *Lettie* and hang out with Garrett. To save time, I took the shortcut through the back field that was home to a pig, which I usually avoided because of the smell. And because the pig must have weighed about four hundred pounds and scared the bejesus out of me.

I know pigs don't eat people, but that thing was a monster. I had no doubt it was only a matter of time before he rammed down the rickety wooden fence that contained him and went on a rampage. Picking my way around the sty, careful not to make eye contact with the pig in case that angered him, I was almost out of the danger zone when I noticed something most unusual.

Ashling was crouched down just outside the fence, obscured almost completely by the giant trough, devouring something hot pink and fluffy. Was that . . . ? Yep. The other one was still in the packaging she clutched in her other hand. It was a Hostess Sno Ball.

My jaw dropped. She froze, a little bit of cream filling on her lip, and stared, like a deer caught in the headlights. I stared back. I couldn't have been more surprised if she'd been shooting up intravenous drugs. I mean, *talk* about historically inaccurate.

"You've, um, got a little something." I pointed to my upper lip. She wiped off the cream, still mute. "Yeah, you got it." I walked over to her and crouched down to her level. She watched me warily, like she thought I was going to sound the accuracy alarm and get the history police running in here. "Can I have some?" Wordlessly, she broke off a pink, coconutty morsel and handed it to me. *"Mmm-mmm."* I swallowed. "Wow, I haven't had one of these in forever. They're good, aren't they? I'd forgotten." Still silent, she nodded. "Thanks." I beamed and stood up, brushing the dirt off my skirt. "We should have started these little snack times earlier in the summer."

Swinging my arms, I strolled jauntily away to the homestead. Could I have ratted her out? Sure. Could I have gloated? A lot? Yeah. Would it have felt good? Probably. But somehow this felt even better.

Once I made it to the homestead, I took the stairs two at a

time, changing as quickly as possible. I ran down to the *Lettie,* but Garrett was nowhere to be found. After reading for a while on deck, I watched the sun set, then headed downstairs to hang out in my bunk.

"Hey." Garrett walked into the fo'c's'le, flung his bag on his bunk, and clambered up after it.

"Hi." I smiled brightly. "What's up?"

"There was a major crisis at the paper involving oversold ad space." He shook his head. "What a nightmare. We've been sorting it out all day. I am so glad to be out of that office." He turned to me and smiled. "What are you reading?"

"You don't want to know." I tried to angle the book into the shadow so he couldn't see the cover.

"Now I really want to know." He hopped out of his bunk and started climbing up to mine.

"No, no!" I shrieked. "It's too embarrassing!"

"Libby, let me see!" Laughing, he wrestled the book away from me.

"Nooo," I moaned, collapsing dramatically. "The agony of defeat."

"*His Reluctant Mistress?*" He raised one eyebrow.

"My secret shame." I buried my face in my pillow. "I ran out of books and I just couldn't read *Northanger Abbey* five times in a row, and this was all they had in that stupid intern house except for *The Art of Knot Tying.*"

"Aha," he said with a smirk. "Lady porn."

"It is not lady porn!" I popped up. "It is historical women's fiction!"

He flipped to the back. "Lord Garrett McCaffrey—renowned rake, skilled seducer, and expert spy—has finally met his match. For singer Libby Kelting may have the voice of an angel, but she will be no man's strumpet—no matter how handsome he is!"

"It does not say that!"

"Close enough." He shrugged. "Will you be my strumpet?" he asked sweetly.

"I'll strumpet you!" I hit him with the book.

"I'm pretty sure you can't use that as a verb."

"Don't you dare go all grammar police on me!"

As he started leaning in to kiss me, something clanked outside the fo'c's'le.

"Garrett." I froze. "What was that?"

"I don't know, a raccoon?" He leaned in. "I thought you were going to strumpet me."

More clanging.

"Garrett, I think it's the ghost, and I think he's angry," I whispered, more scared than I wanted to admit. *Clang, clang, clang.* It sounded like the chains used to pull up an anchor. "Oh my God, Garrett, it's the ghost!" I clutched his T-shirt. "It's the ghost, it's the ghost, it's the ghost," I whimpered.

"Libby, it's not a ghost. There are no such things as ghosts. Um, video evidence to the contrary."

"Get it, Garrett, please get the ghost," I pleaded, like it was a spider I wanted him to squish.

"I can't, uh, 'get it' unless you release the kung fu death grip you have on my shirt, Libby."

The door creaked open. I screamed bloody murder and buried my face in Garrett's chest.

"All right, that's it." Garrett pried my fingers away. "If you're not going to strumpet me, I'm going after it." He hopped out of the bunk. I could hear the ghost clanging away down the hall. Garrett picked up the video camera and took off.

"Oh, don't leave me," I moaned, hopping out of the bunk. "Don't leave me alone in here! I'm coming!"

I caught up with Garrett instantly. The ghost had a head start but was slower than he had been before, probably because of the chains he was carrying. Which made me think that Garrett was right, and the ghost was definitely human. He was still creepy, though. So I looked down as I ran, concentrating on the ghost's shoes, because shoes weren't scary, shoes are my favorites, and shoes . . . the ghost's shoes . . .

"That's no ghost!" I shouted. "He's wearing right and left shoes!"

"Libby, what the hell are you talking about?! What other kind of shoes would he wear?!" Garrett shouted as we sped after the ghost's retreating back.

"Different shoes for right and left feet weren't invented until 1818," I said, panting. Man, this boat was big. We'd circled back around and were running through the galley again. Would we *ever* run out of space in the hold to keep chasing this stupid nonghost? "And they didn't become widespread until the 1850s! This ghost was supposed to have died in 1804. So that's no ghost!"

"Well, that's just great, Libby, but we still need to catch it!"

I had a sudden brainstorm. Ultimate Frisbee. The one remotely athletic thing Garrett had ever mentioned he'd been involved in.

"Garrett! Plate!" I picked up a pewter plate off the end of

the table in the galley. I handed it to Garrett, who tossed it expertly. He hit the ghost right in the back of the knee, causing it to trip.

"Jesus *Christ!*" the ghost shrieked as it toppled over, collapsing in a heap of chains and tumbling to the floor. Garrett and I skidded to a halt in front of it. The ghost moaned and righted itself, slumping miserably into a seated position.

"*Cam?!*" I said incredulously. "What on earth are you *doing?*"

"Haunting." He gestured to his white sailor suit, powdered face, and the chains draped over his arms.

"Yeah, I see that. Um, *why?*"

"Roger's paying me." He shrugged, setting off another round of clanking.

"Roger?!" I asked, stunned. "As in Camden Harbor publicist Roger?"

"Yeah," Cam confirmed. "Nobody knows these ships better than me. So I get two hundred bucks a week to 'haunt' the *Lettie Mae*. That's a nice supplement to my paycheck. And a boat's not cheap, you know. There are ladies in every harbor up and down the Maine coast who need a piece of the Cam-man. That's a lot of sail time. It adds up. Especially in this economy."

"God, you're gross." I shook my head in disgust.

"It makes sense." Garrett nodded thoughtfully. He caught sight of my face. "No, not the ladies-in-every-harbor-Cam-man thing," he clarified. "Roger. You've got to admit, it's a little unorthodox, but he's doing a hell of a job as a publicist. Attendance has nearly tripled since this ghost stuff started."

"Just doing my part to help." Cam flashed us a cocky grin.

"Just doing your part to make quick buck, you mean," I said. "How's the nose?" His grin transformed instantly into a scowl.

"This is going to be huge." Garrett pulled his cell phone out of his back pocket.

"What's going to be huge?" Cam asked nervously.

"The story." Garrett took a quick cell phone picture of Cam in his chains. "I want it ready to go to press tomorrow."

"Dude, you can't publish this story."

"If you didn't want me to write it, then you probably shouldn't have been running around the boat draped in iron chains. Brilliant move, by the way," Garrett said sarcastically. "I can publish it, and I will."

"Come on, man, I'm gonna look like a jackass!" Cam clanked unhappily.

"Frankly," Garrett said brusquely, "I have no problem making you look like a jackass."

"He's right, Garrett—you can't publish it," I whispered.

"What?" Garrett whirled around to face me.

"Thank you, babe." Cam grinned.

"Shut up, Casper, this has nothing to do with you," I snapped. "Garrett, think about what this'll do to the museum."

"It'll give them more publicity," he said stubbornly.

"Not in a good way, and you know it," I argued. "Think about it. Unmasking a publicity stunt like this, orchestrated by a prominent member of the museum staff, will destroy any shred of credibility the museum has! No one will take it seriously anymore. You'll kill the museum."

"Libby, listen to me," he pleaded. "If I do this well, there's a chance a bigger newspaper might pick up the story. I might even get a shot at a national byline. A *national byline.* Maybe even something really big. Like the *New York Times.* The *Times,* Libby. It's what I've always dreamed of." His eyes took on a faraway look. "Do you have any idea what this could do for my career?"

"Do you have any idea what this could do to your town?" I said angrily, eyes flashing. "If the museum shuts down, you will destroy, literally, the lives of everyone you grew up with." He made a noise like he didn't believe me. "Garrett, look at me. You know I'm right. The museum is the main reason people come to this little town, and without the tourist industry, everything in this town will go out of business. *Everything.*"

"I have a responsibility to print the truth." He looked away from me. "That's what reporters do. It's our *job.* There's nothing more important than printing the truth. I can't compromise my journalistic integrity."

"Journalistic integrity? Don't you dare try to take the high road with me," I snapped. "This isn't about journalistic integrity and you know it. This is about your precious *byline,*" I spat out. "God, I thought I knew you. The real you." I shook my head. "I don't know you at all."

"If you did know me at all, you wouldn't stand in my way," he said resolutely. My heart sank. Turned out he was just as smug and self-important as I'd thought he was when we first met. Only he was worse—I hadn't known then that he had no heart. How could he do something that was just so . . . wrong? So purely, horribly selfish?

"Fine. Look, Garrett. I'm not in your way." I gestured to the empty hallway leading down to the way out of the boat. After a brief, angry pause, he stormed out and off the boat.

"Now that he's out of the way . . ." Cam raised an eyebrow. "We've finally got the place all to ourselves."

"Oh, get the hell off my boat," I barked. "Or I really will break your nose this time."

Cam shrugged, clanking. "Well, it was worth a shot." I picked up the pewter plate from where it had fallen at my feet and chucked it at his head. "Ow, Libby, ow!" he whined, deflecting the plate with his arms. "I'm going, I'm going." He left hastily, clanking all the way down the gangplank, and I was left alone in the belly of the ship.

I couldn't sleep. I didn't sleep. Not a wink all night. I moved onto the deck to watch the sun rise, hugging my knees to my chest and wondering how something that seemed so good could have gone so wrong so quickly.

On my way to work, I called Dev. Screw the cell phone rule. I was done with Camden Harbor. Quickly, trying not to cry, I explained the situation.

"Well, screw him!" Dev yelled over the phone. "You are so out of his league, it's not even funny. He effed up the best thing that ever would have happened to him! Let's skip town."

"Really?" I sniffled.

"Really. I'm thinking . . . Quebec," he decided. "You, me, and some French-speaking hotties. I'll make it work. Go clean up your homestead thingy, and I'll pick you up this afternoon."

"Okay." I sniffled again. Dev had already hung up, ostensibly to set plans in motion. My parents probably wouldn't be too pleased about me running away to Canada, but by the time the news reached them in the cell phone dead zone known as Moose Lake, I'd probably be back on my way to Minnesota.

"Libby." Parasol in hand, Ashling—or rather, Susannah Fennyweather—was waiting for me outside the gate to the Bromleigh Homestead. "Hey, Ash, er, Miss Fennyweather," I said, trying to be accommodating.

"No, Ashling's fine." She scuffed the toe of her boot along the fence. "Well, I had a long talk with Martin after . . . after what, um, happened yesterday." She couldn't quite bring herself to say the words *Sno Ball*. But I knew what she meant. "And, well, this summer, if . . . if I came off as overly harsh, I'm sorry," she muttered quickly, and very quietly, all in one breath.

My jaw dropped. "Oh, um, that's okay." I was so shocked, I could barely string together a sentence.

"I just . . . I just take this really seriously. It means a lot to me."

"I understand. History means a lot to me too."

"I know that now, I think." She nodded slowly. "We just see things differently, and I thought that meant you didn't care about any of this and wouldn't take it seriously, but I think maybe you just care about it differently. Anyway," she said, shrugging, "Martin thought I should talk to you about this."

"Martin seems really nice."

"He is." She smiled, and it transformed her whole face. I think it was the first time I'd seen her smile all summer. "And he reminded me that nobody's perfect."

We grinned, both thinking the same, hot pink, coconut-covered thought.

"We'll have to keep in touch," she said. "Listen, are you on Facebook?"

I couldn't have been more surprised if she'd asked me if I was into S-M. I assured her that I was (into Facebook, that is, not S-M), and we parted on somewhat neutral terms, having reached a fragile peace. I watched Ashling go, like Italy in 1915, having joined the Allied forces against all the odds. Well, stranger things had happened.

Even with the Ashling truce, I spent a miserable day, sweeping, dusting, and washing—waiting for the minutes to tick by until the afternoon rolled around and Dev would come rescue me.

"Well, what do you know." Dev walked into the homestead, sipping from something that looked like a Frappuccino with an enormous dollop of whipped cream. "Pilgrims *do* wear pink."

I looked down at my favorite pink flowered dress. "Like I said, Dev, not a pilgrim."

SLAP. The *Camden Crier* hit the table in front of me.

"I'm not going to read that, Dev."

"Read it, Libby," he said seriously. I kept wiping the table. "Libby. Look at me." I did. Dev was more solemn than maybe I'd ever seen him. "I am asking you, as your friend, to please at least look at the article."

"Fine. Okay? Fine. Whatever." He *had* to play the friend card. I huffily flipped it open, searching for Garrett's byline. Oddly enough, it was buried way in the back, in a small paragraph at the bottom of the page. I hastily skimmed the article: " . . . several different sightings . . . blah, blah, blah . . . Can neither confirm nor deny veracity of reports of paranormal activity . . . blah, blah, blah . . . Perhaps some things are better left a mystery."

Stunned, I looked to Dev for answers.

"He didn't write the article." He shrugged.

"He didn't write the article," I whispered, tears in my eyes.

Something Madam Selena had said came back to me: "Love is a force that makes you choose and decide." Garrett had chosen. And now it was my turn.

"You know what that means, don't you?" Dev said as he slurped up a blob of Frappuccino. "That six-foot-two bundle of dork—"

"Loves me," I finished for him. "He loves me," I said breathlessly, beaming.

"I was gonna say 'wants your cookies,' but sure, that'll work too."

"I have to find him." I started banging cabinets open, recklessly flinging about cleaning supplies so I could leave the homestead. "Do you know where he is?" I asked as I put away the last of the dishrags.

"He was at Camden Coffee, downtown, when I got my Caramel-Coco-Choco-Mocha-Nutaccino, extra whipped. Dunno if he's still there, though . . ." Dev trailed off.

I stopped and stared at him, stricken.

"Go." Dev sighed, exasperated. "Go get your man! I'll clean up here." I gawked. "Yes, you heard me right, I offered to clean." He rolled his eyes. "Now *go*."

"Thank you, Dev!" I called as I hitched up my skirts.

"Run, Libby, run!" he shouted.

The kitchen door slammed behind me, and I was off. I sprinted through the garden gate, down the lane, and out of the museum grounds, running down the sidewalk toward downtown Camden Harbor. Cars honked at the crazy blond chick in colonial dress, but I didn't care. I just needed to make it to that coffee shop as fast as humanly possible. Around the time I passed the CVS, I got a second wind and practically flew down Main Street, past the Dairy Bar, the toy store, and a lot of very confused tourists. I skidded to a stop in front of Camden Coffee's large front windows but instead of stopping, I just kept skidding, until I pitched forward and fell flat on my face. My palms scraped against the sidewalk, and my petticoats ballooned up around my waist. As I tried to gather myself up, flopping around on the sidewalk, I heard the bell tinkle as someone opened the door to the coffee shop. I struggled to a sitting position and looked up.

Garrett was standing above me, book in hand.

"I fell," I said. It was sort of self-evident. But it just popped out of my mouth.

"I can see that." Garrett crouched down to join me and gingerly reached over with his free hand to push a curl out of my eyes. "I didn't catch you."

"I don't—I don't need you to catch me," I said, and as I spoke the words aloud, I realized they were true. I didn't need a hero. Or a rescuer. Or someone to catch me when I fell or to sweep me off my feet. I'd been chasing this dream of a fairy-tale romance, only to find that so much of what I thought I'd wanted was an illusion. I knew now that I didn't need a hero. I just needed him.

"I know you don't need me to catch you." Garrett took my hand and turned it over. My right palm was bleeding where I'd broken my fall. "I probably couldn't, anyway. I'm pretty uncoordinated." He set his book down, reached into his pocket, and pulled out a Band-Aid. As he unwrapped it, I realized with a shock that it had Hello Kitty printed on it.

"Hello Kitty Band-Aids?" I squeaked out. "Did you—did you get those for me?"

"No, they're mine," he deadpanned. "Of course they're for you. I've been carrying them around for weeks. Libby, within two minutes of our meeting, you fell in a barrel. I was pretty sure it was only a matter of time before you fell again." He tenderly stuck the Band-Aid over my cut. "Maybe I can't catch you. But I can help you pick yourself up when you fall." His hand lingered over mine. "You don't need me to catch you or to fight your battles, Wonder Woman. Cam learned that the hard way." He grinned, clearly relishing the memory of when I'd punched Cam at the ball. "That's one of the things I like most about you. To name just one of a million."

I blushed, looked down, and noticed the cover of his book.

"Is that—is that *Northanger Abbey*?" I knew he'd borrowed it, but I couldn't believe he'd actually read it. Just because I'd said it was my favorite.

He nodded. "Just finished it. I have to say, I didn't much care for it."

"Um, okay, I—what? Why?"

"I couldn't stand the way Henry was always lecturing Catherine, talking about how ignorant women are, and going on and on and *on* about politics and landscaping and all sorts of random crap." He ran his hands through his hair, messy as ever. "I think, in the end, Henry Tilney actually learned a hell of lot more from Catherine than she learned from him." He smiled wryly, tentatively.

Was this a metaphor? Was I Catherine? Was he Henry? Did this mean . . . ?

"Catherine learned a lot from Henry too," I said carefully. "Catherine made a lot of mistakes. A lot. She was wrong about almost everything." I looked up nervously into his eyes, afraid that I'd made too many mistakes. Afraid that it was too late. But I saw nothing in his soft brown eyes but warmth.

"Henry made a lot of mistakes too," he said gently. "But in the end, he finally got it right."

"You didn't write the article," I blurted out.

"I couldn't do it." He shrugged. "Libby, you care about the museum. And I care about you," he said simply. "Once I thought about it, it was the easiest decision I've ever made."

I could feel myself light up. Garrett was better than Mr. Darcy, Rhett Butler, and Henry Tilney combined. Because he was real. And now I knew that he really, truly cared about me. And that feeling was worth a thousand sonnets.

"You know," I said, glowing, "a very wise psychic once told me that love is a force that makes us choose and decide."

"All that paranormal astrology stuff is ridiculous," he said dismissively. "But just this once"—his tone softened—"that very wise psychic is right."

He leaned in, and there, right there, sitting on the sidewalk, in the dirt, on Main Street, Camden Harbor, in perhaps the least romantic spot in the universe, Garrett kissed me.

I didn't know if I believed in "happily ever after" anymore. I mean, I didn't know what would happen tomorrow, let alone for forever and ever after. But I did know that I was happy, right there, right then, with him.

And that was all I needed to know.

THE END

ACKNOWLEDGMENTS

Two years ago I was an actress with a blog who never imagined I'd have a book published. Without all of these people, I never would have.

Thanks to my amazing editor Amanda and the Doe Coover team for taking a chance on me, and for all your help throughout multiple revisions. Thanks to my fantastic editor Bethany Vinhateiro and everyone at HMH and Graphia for bringing *Pilgrims* to life, and for ridding it of all the unnecessary em dashes.

Thanks to my Spice Girls, my Dreamgirls, and my Sex and the Valley girls—you make me laugh and keep me sane. Thanks to all my friends who read my stuff in its early days—you guys are the reason I kept writing. Thanks to the Pepper to my Salt for inspiration, to Caitlin for understanding the importance of cake time, and to Lorelei the wonder pup for snuggles. Max, when I started writing *Pilgrims,* I never imagined I'd have a boyfriend even better than Garrett by the time it was published, but apparently miracles do happen. Thank you for everything.

Thanks to my little sister, who gave this book her hard-won approval; to Mom, who didn't even need to read it to know she loved it; and to Dad, who read every word I ever wrote, every step of the way.

AR Level _4.7_

Points _8.0_

Lexile _HL720L_